MALICE OF SNOW

Malice of Snow
Book 1 in the First Crown series

C. Higgins

First published in Great Britain by C. Higgins in 2018

This edition published by Askaria Publishing

Second Edition

ISBN 9781796591521

callumhiggins.site123.me

[Find the official maps at callumhiggins.site123.me/the-maps]

https://www.facebook.com/chigginsofficial/

CHAPTER 1
MALICE OF SNOW

Borgian Steel was saddled up on horseback, his horse was a proud, jet-black steed that he had hired from the nearest city of Sesan, ruled over by Clan Crewe.

The stallion reared its head to face the colds of the place they traversed: a snow-speckled, freezing borough known as the Cold.

The Cold was one of five boroughs in a land known as Askaria, the Land of Kings, a place where cities were ruled by clans: great families that had resulted from the evolution of the first Askarian Tribes of Gorl.

It had been 59 years since the Arch King, who had illegalised magic, Corpulus Adermino's death and since, two clans had fought a war of bloodshed and fury with revenge and power on their minds.

The First Crown was what all strived for, what every man and woman craved, the symbol of the King of Askaria forged by the first civilisation, and to only reveal itself to those deemed worthy by the crown or those decided eligible by the Council Moot of Askaria—a group of three whose job was electing the next heir.

A cold breeze made Borgian shiver.

Borgian was an ex-bandit, he had made his friends and enemies, plundered gold and served his time in an elven prison, he was a man of 34 years in age and had a spirit like most of his in Askaria;

brave, good-hearted but not without a lust for power, hidden beneath the surface.

He rode into a collection of trees which shrouded a large instalment of rocky cliff known as Hagmars wall.

The frigid wind bounded past Borgian's pale ears, covered slightly by his bedhead-like black hair which sat atop his ruggedly handsome face, occupied by grey-silver eyes and a chin decorated with stubble which matched the features, that looked like they had been carved by a master, onto his face.

His friend, Lasgot Dehrimin, accompanied him.

Lasgot was friendly, charming and an ex-bandit like Borgian.

Lasgot had come into the business of banditry when his family exiled him to the wilds after committing thievery in the city of Hernight and bringing shame to his family name.

They had both hailed from the Bandit's Triangle in the north-west of Askaria and had recently abandoned their previous lives due to a power struggle arising between the camps of the triangle.

The Bandit's Triangle was formed of three camps; Tanlor, Ralruff and the most powerful camp that all paid tribute to, the Kalgyyr camp.

Borgian and Lasgot had plundered as much as they could from their camp, the Tanlor camp, behind everyone's backs, before escaping.

If Borgian and Lasgot were to return near the Triangle now, they would be hunted without mercy for thievery and abandonment.

They were rogues now, lone wolves, and spent their days looking for treasure and artefacts; it was their last resort since there were no other lives for them.

It was all they could do, living out each day in the hopes of finding something that could restore them to some sort of power.

"Remind me Borgian, why are we out in the bloody freezing, windswept lands of Askaria's coldest wilds when we could be—'nother mind," Lasgot cut himself off, remembering they had nowhere to return to and nobody to accept them in, with their current reputations.

"We are out here for the same reason you didn't finish that sentence and for another reason, to end the tension between clans that slowly destroys this land," Borgian replied with irritation in his voice.

Even as Borgian said it, he felt himself cringe.

He was truly seeking the impossible, nothing could possibly end the war between Clan Alok and Clan Herginn.

"Oh, you mean the fairy tale," Lasgot fought to make himself heard over the sound of the strong winds.

"Not a fairy tale, Lasgot, arguing the Sword of Fading doesn't exist is like saying the First Crown doesn't symbolise kingship, and the map I hold should lead us to the knight and the sword's location."

"The First Crown?" Lasgot burst out in disbelief, "this land no longer cares for the crown or any other instrument of power, Mazdol Herginn and Zensi Alok pretend they care for the crown, maybe they did, but they probably just want to rip each other's throats out at this point."

"You used to have faith, Lasgot, in this land, what's possible for it."

"I see Zensi and Mazdol and I wonder if this land's possibilities are still able to make everyone's favour," Lasgot looked dismal.

"Possibility will never make everyone's favour, it's just luck that it reaches the people that deserve it."

"Huh, luck..."

"How about you be quiet for the time being, I don't want your disbelief to touch me at this point. I can feel we're close."

Borgian was ignoring Lasgot now, looking ahead, he stayed silent and was for the rest of the trip down the off-road route.

Horses hooves sounded clip-clopping as they trotted on—until they came to a halt.

They reared up, whinnying.

Borgian and Lasgot were thrown off their saddles, into the mud.

The horses backed up onto their hind legs before returning to their four-legged pose and cantering backwards.

Borgian quickly rolled out the way so not to be trampled, he watched his horse trod back and then stop.

Borgian slowly found his feet so as not to startle the horse any further and, holding and stroking the steed's head, tried to calm her.

Lasgot stood, frozen, in the face of what lay ahead.

"Shh, shh," Borgian re-mounted his horse before turning his head around to face the scene that had entranced Lasgot, the trees and bushes around the area were not only turning a frosty blue but were freezing, crisping ... dying.

"What is this?" Borgian asked himself as he dismounted his horse once more and proceeded to push the shrubbery apart.

Lasgot followed him.

They were at the face of Hagmars Wall now and a small pit in the ground lay before them, that was where the icy aura seemed to be protruding from.

It was like a smog, a mist.

"Down we go, then," Borgian braced himself to jump but was held back by Lasgot.

"Don't be an idiot Borgian, you don't know how far that goes down."

Lasgot ignited one of many torches he carried in his saddle sack, it didn't fall far, the light of the torch was clearly visible.

"A jump? At most, I'll break a leg," Borgian detached his armoured chest plate from his torso so that he could jump without restraint.

Borgian gave Lasgot a smirk, "You coming?"

Lasgot followed him hesitantly as they jumped together.

The floor was crunchy, like grass on a frosty morning.

The smog seemed to come from a dark, stretching tunnel within.

Lasgot retrieved the dropped torch, "What do you expect to find here, Borgian, what if this is just simply a hole in the ground? What if you've doomed us and we never get out of here?"

Borgian looked at his doubting friend, "Look at the way these tunnels are carved out, these aren't natural formations."

"And so, you believe that people would spend their time digging out this hole?" Lasgot inquired.

"Well, yes, under the right influence."

"I don't know, maybe there is something more to this," Lasgot paused, "but either way, I don't like it down here, the mist is strange, unnatural, there's more to this than meets the eye."

"I'll admit, the mist ... it is eerie but still, we must focus on the Sword of Fading, that is what is truly more to this and when we find it, you'll wonder why in hell you didn't like it, or the idea of it at least."

The mist seemed to begin to get thicker the further they proceeded in, till Borgian could only make out a rough outline of his companion.

The next thing to hit them both was the distinct smell of smoke.

The two began to choke uncontrollably and soon enough, Lasgot started coughing up blood—just as they reached an interesting scene.

"Look at it," Borgian directed Lasgot to a huge circular stone door decorated with strange symbols and covered in a sheet of dripping, melting ice.

"How do we open it?" Lasgot wondered aloud.

"There's your curious spirit," Borgian grinned as he began feeling various places on the door.

"No, it isn't, it's the fact that I'm coughing up blood! Hopefully, this is a way out."

Lasgot helped Borgian with the door and after scraping some of the ice off of the surface, found a circular rune plate.

"Borgian, I think I've found something."

Borgian walked over and looked at what Lasgot had discovered.

Borgian pushed it with both hands and the plate started to glow blue, the door shook open, splitting in the centre.

"How has no one found this before?" Lasgot walked behind Borgian, talking.

A scraping sound echoed through the dark area.

"Shh," Borgian tried to get Lasgot quiet as he lit another torch to get a knowledge of what the sound was.

Amber light lit up the whole chamber and, in the middle, with his arms attached with chains to huge cogs, was a knight—literally in shining armour, standing completely frozen, glistening in a ray of sunlight escaping from a hole in the ground, directly above.

The knight's face was that of a skeleton's and what looked like sweat somehow dripped down his skull.

The origins of the smoke came from four huge braziers spitting blue sparks from their blue fires.

Borgian and Lasgot put out their torches, seeing that there was no longer a need for them.

"Is he alive?" Lasgot asked dumbly, even as he saw the knight was but an ancient skeleton.

Borgian answered the question by walking up to the knight and looking at it for a moment before touching it on the head, it didn't move, "I doubt it."

And yet the scraping sound seemed to emit from the knight's hollowed mouth.

"An undead perhaps."

In front of the knight, on a stone altar-like table, lay the brilliant blue frost-covered sapphire longsword, the Sword of Fading.

"Lasgot, I believe we have found the Blue Knight, with his sword, we can put an end to the scourges that destroy this world," Borgian smiled, "with this, we can control the Malice of Snow, become lords, kings, take up the First Crown," Borgian walked over to the knight.

"Careful Borgian, nothing's ever easy in this land," Lasgot warned.

Borgian nodded and approached the blade, "Well, we'll see."

Borgian then picked up the blade, a cold seemed to seep into his soul, Borgian shivered.

"Borgian? Are you okay?"

Borgian was silent for a moment before he announced, "It's god damn cold."

The two both laughed but their moment of rejoicing was cut short.

The table moved below the ground suddenly, breaking where the chains met and revealing the ends which sped off into the cogs holding them, that began to turn around fast.

The shackles holding the knight froze and then broke, the chains were released from their place in the cogs.

The fires burnt out and the Blue Knight slowly started to move.

He could be seen in the small amount of light peering from a hole in the ground above.

He faced Borgian and Lasgot.

And then, a burning pain struck Borgian's hand, he dropped the blade and clutched his wrist.

He looked at his hand and there was a symbol there, burnt into his flesh, a symbol of two crossed lines with a circle enveloping them.

Rolgirtis retrieved the blade as layers of skin began to form over his skull.

He proceeded to take the helmet from off the table and equipped it, his cloudy blue eyes glowed in the shadows through his helmet's eyeholes.

"Borgian 'Steel' Veles," the Blue Knight talked, his voice was thin and cold yet strangely human considering the thousand or so years he had been in a dead-trance sleep for.

From out of the symbol engraved in Borgian's right hand, a blue light spread and attached itself to Rolgirtis' blade.

"King Rolgirtis the Blue Knight is bound with his sword once more as you now are, too," Rolgirtis announced once more in a third person, singsong sort of way.

"What have you done?" Borgian asked, still gripping the painful engraving in his hand.

"I bound you to the snow and now your soul is but a vessel for me to feed upon. When the sign pains you, when you feel your soul riving in your skin, you will know of my hunger," Rolgirtis explained simply, "I thank you for your submission and now I depart. I've been dead for too long and now the time has come to shape this new world, with your kind here to witness it."

Rolgirtis his left sword-less hand towards the hole in the ground above them, and a staircase of solid ice manifested.

Rolgirtis mounted it and something reckless inside of Borgian made him follow, he also somehow managed to mount the icy stairs with ease.

Borgian and Lasgot succeeded in reaching the ground, in enough time to see the Blue Knight, Rolgirtis, summon a steed from the snow of the ground.

He whisked his sword in the air, knocking Borgian back and was off.

Borgian quickly mounted his own horse.

"Are you crazy!" Lasgot shouted.

"Lasgot, I fear if we do not catch up, Askaria is doomed," Borgian replied with worry etched on his face.

Lasgot jumped on his white steed, which had regained its calm, and the two were off.

CHAPTER 2
All HAIL CLAN HERGINN

The doors to the longhouse of Talgrin city swung open.

"All hail Clan Herginn," a soldier dressed in blood red, boiled leather armour with the insignia of the black boar and dagger—representing the ruling family of Talgrin city, Clan Herginn, announced.

"What is the meaning of this interruption, I was talking with my son, do you have news of my dau—"

Mazdol Herginn looked up and saw his daughter.

"Ah, there you are, Ariesa," Mazdol then diverted his attention back to the soldier, "where was she?"

"We found her out at the Forgemaster's Path, the path leading from here to Mezal city,"

Mazdol took in a deep breath before shouting out, "What do you not understand about not leaving the city and to go out to visit our enemy, Clan Alok are our enemy, Mezal city homes our enemy, I will not have you going there, not now, not ever!"

Ariesa Herginn blushed like a beetroot with a look of loss in her eyes.

"It's him, isn't it, it's Zensi's son, Frienz, well, isn't it, we have been feuding with Clan Alok for about sixteen years and you wish to give yourself freely to their son," he huffed, "after all I've done for you, you run out the doors of my city to mingle with the heir of Clan Alok, do you forget our saying 'in blood is forged our eternal flame' , in our own pure blood and the blood of our enemies, the boy is not worthy of you and my mind is set. You will marry your brother,

Stork, and rule over this great city of Talgrin with him when I die," Mazdol finished.

"Father, why did you kill Marcus Alok," Ariesa asked inquisitively and rudely, suddenly changing the subject.

"Marcus Alok killed your grandfather and my father, Arcturus ... I had waited too long after my father's death and vengeance was overdue."

"But did you ever think about Zensi? Marcus was her father, did she deserve to go through what you did? If you didn't kill Marcus, you wouldn't be in this feud, and did you ever think about us?"

"Do not question my methods, daughter, I wouldn't have today any different," he told Ariesa as she walked to her room.

"She must marry her brother, the purity of my clan must stay ripe," Mazdol signalled a guard, "place your men at the gates, ensure she doesn't leave."

The guard, as he left, muttered the words, "All hail Clan Herginn."

"Come on, we're right on his tail!" Borgian shouted out to his faithful companion, Lasgot.

They were approaching Hagmars wall again, but this time, the back of it.

The Blue Knight suddenly halted, his horse turned back into the snow of the ground and he placed one hand out, his palm facing forward.

The horses that Lasgot and Borgian were riding on, turned to ice and were thrown to the trees where they smashed into thousands of pieces.

Borgian recovered himself from the ground to see the Blue Knight plunge the Sword of Fading into the ground.

"Right on my tail? What do you hope to achieve? I can't kill you yet, that would be a waste, so—" Rolgirtis raised his blade and Borgian began writhing in pain, clutching at the symbol lighting up on his hand.

"The Malice of Snow has awakened due to your own idiocy and greed, and nothing will stop it. If you're so eager to know of what it can do then head to the nearest city and spectate true power."

Lasgot went to attack Rolgirtis but when Lasgot had found his feet again, he saw that he and Borgian were now on the outskirts of the woods surrounding Hagmars Wall.

The powers to transport people and to turn animals to ice with a movement of his wrist: Rolgirtis was already too well equipped and he had only just started feeding, gaining his powers from Borgian's soul.

Borgian was connected to this demon now.

"I didn't expect it to be easy."

CHAPTER 3
FAMILY OF ALOK

"What news do you bring?" Countess Zensi Alok, who bore the symbol of the black Askarian Kingbird of her clan, on her green banners asked, "has my son been found?"

"No, Countess, Frienz has not been found, I have my best men out there, so there is no need to worry."

"Worry is an understatement, I fear, I imagine every scenario that could have befallen him, and with Ariesa Herginn, I know love when I see it but I worry for his welfare. Mazdol is dangerous and Frienz is the product of my blood and arcane magic too, I am yet to find out how that effects, no father to have given a real product for his birth."

The captain of the guard nodded his head and left out the giant spruce doors.

Zensi huffed.

She looked to another one of her soldiers, "Bring me the Godspeaker, Georlia."

The soldier was off, his footsteps sounded, heavy, as he walked to a door on the right side of Zensi.

The soldier whispered something inside the room and almost instantly, a small, old blind woman, wearing a brown robe and a silver ring embedded with a single jet, appeared before Zensi.

"My Countess, you requested me."

"Indeed, I did, I need you to consult my future, the loss of my father still haunts me, and I wish to know, will I ever avenge him."

"Why now? Why again?"

Zensi gave a puzzled look.

"You have made me see that same future of yours every time you have requested me for such things, I must know ... Why so persistent?" Georlia explained her thoughts.

"Mazdol grows stronger every day, even as he cowers in his stronghold of a city, luck always seems to find him, and he never need lift a finger to attract that luck, why would luck favour a man so vile and merciless, dishonest and unfeeling? Maybe my future holds some light to shine on this," Zensi stood up out of her throne, "men who would kill the mothers of children and the fathers of mothers deserve only pain, when that pain comes, is what I need to know."

Georlia tried to imagine her strong woman master before her, in her mind's eye.

She managed to see her, worthy of all respects, and a throne, a queendom and a crown.

Georlia's moon-white eyes scanned the scene before her.

She could sense soldiers and advisors speckled around the courtroom.

"Meet me at the temple—somewhere more private."

The Temple of Kinsia was an old building, one that had been defaced in war and burnt down twice.

Zensi always had to remark about how it had survived past the rest of the buildings in Mezal after all that it had gone through.

She entered inside, dismissing her group of bodyguards.

As she entered, she saw a couple of priestesses of Kinsia flee away from the ceremony room as Georlia finished a sentence.

"Why did you wish to commence the ceremony here?" Zensi questioned, "why not in the comfort of the courtroom, like the rest of my prophecies?"

"Because, today won't be like the rest, my Countess, too long have we only seen small pieces of a bigger board game, too long have these pieces been neglected and so we must, today, lay them all out on the board."

"But you still haven't explained to me why you have decided not to do this in front of my advisors."

"Because, this ceremony requires the illegal, that of which was banned by our last king," Georlia spoke in a meaningful, solid tone, "we must invoke the powers of the arcane."

Zensi looked at Georlia, "I trust you, Georlia, anything to make sure I know how to combat my future, to kill Mazdol."

"Good," Georlia placed a sinister looking box on the floor, it was made from darkened silver and engraved with jets and rubies, "these boxes were used by seers all the time when magic was still legal, they carry the blood of the seer and the one who's prophecy is to be read."

"And then..."

"Then you enter my mind, see what I see, enter another world, are you ready?"

Zensi nodded, "Yes."

"Then take this dagger and draw blood from your right hand."

Zensi did as commanded, hesitantly.

Blood dripped from her palm, into the box.

The rubies glowed.

Georlia took the knife from Zensi and then dug it into her own hand.

The jets lit up as the blood dripped into the box.

18

Zensi looked to Georlia for further instructions but Georlia suddenly fell to the floor.

Zensi quickly rushed over to her side, she rolled Georlia onto her back but jumped back quickly, when she saw that Georlia's skin had been peeled off to reveal a skeleton of ice.

"Help, somebody help!" Zensi called out.

It took Zensi a few minutes to get up but when she did, she made her way out of the temple, the sight that she beheld was her city frozen, the bricks replaced with solid ice.

Zensi couldn't talk; she was fearful, confused.

She walked among the structures of ice and noticed that they were beginning to melt.

Blood and rotting entrails sweated from the ice, causing Zensi to cup her right hand over her nose, attempting to stifle the smell.

And then ... masses of people dressed in green armour, but there was something wrong with them, their skin was bluish-green and stretched over their faces like masks.

Zensi went running the other way but the same came from the other direction, just dressed in red.

She spotted Mazdol, he was part of the red infected.

The buildings began to lean, and dragons flew overhead, they spewed fire over the city.

She headed towards Mazdol, she glanced at his ill face before he disintegrated, his body in ashes...

Dragons flew away from their position in the sky and then, so did the armies disappear.

All that was left was an iron crown with green emeralds embedded in it.

Zensi went to fetch it but before her eyes, the crown turned red in its gems, and the ashes, they reformed.

Mazdol stood before her and then all the clans, families and bandit groups, everyone in Askaria.

They fought.

Zensi was trampled, and then suddenly, she was back in the temple with Georlia standing over her.

"You're alive?" Zensi had to question it, dumbly, "was that my prophecy?"

Georlia had a fearful look on her face.

"I wish I could say it was just yours, but that was all of Askaria's prophecies in one, everyone was there, everything was there, and in that case, we're all doomed."

"What do you mean?"

"The Malice of Snow, the Tears of Fire, the Red King and the Children of Askaria, all legendary events that foretell doom, they were first seen by the master seer, Maegaren Fral and were recorded in the Book of Signs."

"So, what do we?"

"We and everyone else must pray, reconcile, put feuds aside, the end of days is coming."

CHAPTER 4
THE NEAREST CITY

"How much? Name your price," Borgian questioned.

"500 Heads," a fisherman dressed in dyed leather and rags exclaimed.

"Ridiculous, 350," Lasgot negotiated, whilst pulling a disgusted face at the smell of the fishermen's catch, in storage barrels.

"450."

"then we have an accord," Borgian agreed quickly before Lasgot could put another say in.

The fishermen handed over two horses in return for a leather pouch that Borgian revealed

The fisherman shook the pouch, testing it.

"Feels like 450," the fisherman said.

"It *is*," Borgian stated with a slight annoyance as he mounted the horse he had chosen.

"How many more Heads do you have on you?" the fisherman advanced.

"I don't think you are in any place to ask that," Borgian warned, his hand near his sword.

"Nice doing business with you," the fisherman smiled nervously, showing his black, rotten teeth before quickly retreating.

Borgian and Lasgot jumped atop their horses, turned them around and sped off.

"Faster, faster," Borgian Steel called out to the horses, they were departing from the snowy tundra behind and entering the hot grasslands.

"Why are we going so fast?" Lasgot struggled for breath as the wind battered his face.

"I'm guessing you don't know the uncontrolled damage that the Malice of Snow imposes, we need to take cover and alert the city of Sesan and the land of the Benedoecs that surround it, Sesan's the nearest city and is most under threat right now, Rolgirtis warned the Malice of Snow would start its path of destruction there."

The horses were trailing dust behind them as they galloped.

At this point, the horses no longer needed the encouragement to go faster.

They could sense the impending danger.

Fear channelled their speed.

Darkness started to gather above them as night fell on the Land of Askaria, torn apart by spilt blood, ravaged by disease, ripped to pieces by greed, yet for some reason, never susceptible to the continuing destruction but that could all change...

The Malice of Snow had the power to drive races out from very existence and perhaps would be the thing to make Askaria fall.

Soon enough, Borgian Steel and his companion, Lasgot Dehrimin, had arrived at the torch-lit gate of Sesan, its superior stone walls stood to attention with crenellations shielding the tower tops.

Borgian approached a bulky looking soldier with the yellow dog, a symbol of Clan Crewe, imprinted on his armour.

"We need to speak to your lord immediately, it is imperative that we do so," Borgian called out whilst still walking towards Sesan.

The soldier made a movement with his head and without even questioning the two's reason for needing an entrance, he exclaimed: "Yes, of course, let me open the gates."

With a horrible screeching sound, the entrance was open.

"Oh, and I'll need your name," the guard told Borgian.

"Borgian Steel"

The guard nodded, "Welcome to Sesan," the guard didn't recognise Borgian, even with his name, as the infamous ex-bandit.

This surprised him.

Sesan awaited them, marvellously lit with the setting sun, it was filled with small, comfortable shacks and large wooden mansions, tiny corner clubs and welcoming inns, and jewellery stands and blacksmiths, markets and breweries.

"Come Lasgot, we must alert the lord, I have a straight-away liking to this city, it would be a shame to lose it."

Lasgot however, wasn't listening, he was instead eyeing up a blonde woman in a vibrant blue dress, working a brewery store selling sweetberry infused mead—he also seemed to have a straightaway liking to the city.

"Sweetberry infused mead with elderflower residue and wild honey, Hollyburst Meadery's newest casket mead: the Hollyburst Huntsman," she chanted over the market voices.

"How about I leave you here to buy some mead, I don't think listening is your strongest point especially when there's a woman with an exquisite body on her, in the area. Very exquisite..." Borgian teased.

Lasgot gave Borgian a glance and exclaimed, "Hey. She's mine."

Borgian walked away to the longhouse and as he reached the doors, the guards were eager to let him in, it seemed like Sesan was a boring location for the guard who had trained to fight, not stand and watch for people entering and exiting the city.

Borgian entered the longhouse which opened straight into the dining room where the lord was eating.

"Ah, a new visitor to my city, welcome, you must be Borgian, my soldiers alerted me of your arrival, I have been told you needed to see me with a matter of urgency, so what is it."

"My lord, as ridiculous as it may sound to you, the Malice of Snow has been unleashed and I fear it will hit Sesan first, I found the Blue Knight and his sword at Hagmars Wall."

Lord Ulric suddenly looked furious, "The Malice of Snow is not something to joke about, it may have existed, it may have not and how would you even find the Blue Knight? Many have looked for him before and many have come back empty-handed."

Borgian took two long worn pieces of parchment from his pocket and spread them out on the dining table, pushing various dishes aside, they were maps.

"I bought these from a friend who had recently been to Bolgron Island, where the Malice of Snow was believed to have first struck, they come from one of the destroyed White Elv cities there," Borgian pointed to three spots on the map of Bolgron Island, "the three main places where the Malice of Snow hit, it was said that the White Elves overthrew their King, Rolgirtis, and locked him in a place in accordance with these when transacted to Askaria."

Borgian pointed now to Hagmars wall on the Askarian map, "This is the centre of where the three places would be if on Askaria, now do you see? We found him there and he promised destruction here." Borgian finished.

"Carac," Ulric called.

An elderly man appeared and instantly started examining the map, he whispered something in Ulric's ears and then was gone.

"I am sorry for doubting you, Borgian, my historian tells me the map is genuine, thank you for warning me, but still—"

"What?" Borgian exclaimed.

"Nothing."

Ulric presented a ring to Borgian, it was gold with a garnet embedded within it, "A token of my appreciation and please, if you wish to stay, the Sleeping Ox inn has plenty of rooms although, with the knowledge that something such as the Malice of Snow is coming, I don't see why you would want to stay, well, it's been a pleasure meeting you," Ulric then let out a strange noise, fear, Borgian thought.

Borgian took that as his queue to leave.

"Oh, and could you take the back exit, prevents gossip among the people."

"Oh yes, one last thing, I heard your wife had left the city, is she somewhere safe?"

"Leyla? On a trade agreement in The Eye and The Mouth, with those religious bastards, the Missionaries."

"Perhaps in a foreign land, is the best place to be at this time."

Ulric put out his hand, they shook and Borgian left back into the cold air of the outside city, under the setting sun.

Lasgot was waiting for Borgian outside with his lady friend to which, Borgian found out, her name was Emi.

They all headed to the Sleeping Ox inn and Borgian told Lasgot what had happened over a cold pint of the mead Lasgot had bought earlier, Borgian had never tasted anything so good.

The sky turned black and the sun disappeared under the horizon.

This would be the beginning of everything, the last day before judgement.

CHAPTER 5

FOOL'S LOVE

Ariesa Herginn quietly crept out of her bed, from beneath her covers, she tip-toed through her dormitory in her gown, down the stairs.

She had secretly sent a private courier to tell Frienz to meet her at the crossroads out of the city, days ago before she had been recaptured by her father's men.

The hard part of this was escaping her own house to find her love, luckily as a young child restrained by her father at that age too, she had learnt every passageway and corridor leading out of the house, leading out of the city.

She pushed a brick in the wall and a hidden mechanism brought the concrete down into the ground, revealing the door out.

She opened the door which screeched annoyingly loud, she hoped to the gods that nobody had heard her, and then silently sealed the passageway behind her and into the stables, she went.

She mounted a pure white horse and galloped off into the moonlit night, out of the secret stable exit, across the cobbled paths, out of Talgrin city.

And she had done it and Frienz Alok, her Frienz was standing there at the crossroads just as planned.

She dismounted her horse.

He smiled at her arrival.

"I'm so glad to see you or I would be to see anyone out here, I've been walking for about a day out of the city, but I'd do it all again for you."

Ariesa considered whether Frienz' mother would be worried, angry or disgusted like her father.

In the end, she decided just to treasure the time she had with Frienz without any other thoughts defiling this solace.

She sat down with him on a bench and talked to him about her woes and worries.

Bathing in the darkness and peace.

However, it was not long before their harmony was disturbed: the sound of footsteps, metal clanking.

"What is that?" Ariesa asked.

"I don't know," Frienz replied, drawing his sword.

It turned out to be a group of soldiers and when they came closer, the insignia of the black Kingbird on green was apparent, they were soldiers of Clan Alok.

"Lord Frienz, are you alright."

They turned and saw Ariesa, "It's the Herginn girl, capture her."

Frienz tried to push the soldiers off but they continued to bind her in rope.

"Get your hands off her!" Frienz shouted.

"Sorry, we must ensure your safety."

They also began to bind Frienz in rope too.

"If this really is who we think it is, then she and her father may be responsible for Frienz's disappearance and I'm sure Zensi would love to meet the person who would dare make that happen."

One of the soldiers laughed.

Ariesa was hauled onto the carriage like heavy cargo.

She knew where she was going without being told.

She was going to Mezal city, home of Clan Alok.

CHAPTER 6
WAKE THE WINTER'S WOE

A night had passed in Sesan City.

In that night, whilst everyone slept calmly, the weather had taken a dramatic turn.

Sesan was usually sweltering with sunlight but for the first time in approximately fifty years, the sky became dark and snow poured from it like a waterfall of frozen tears from a god.

Everyone was inside their houses except for the beggars and hermits and un-executed outcasts who were shouting out rants and warnings, and the lord's personal wizards began casting their spells of protection.

Borgian left the inn and went outside to see the form from which the noise that had awakened him, sounded.

It came in the many forms previously discussed.

The ranting was the loudest and most annoyingly deterring.

All started to come out of their houses in an instant, to watch the scene unfold in front of them, that rare scene.

Another sound soon entered Borgian's ears.

The noise came from the distance.

It was a sound like rough swaying that entered his eardrums.

Borgian decided it might be best to alert Lasgot and his partner, Emi, as the fear that then began to course through his veins, convinced him of only one explanation for the death call.

The Malice of Snow had awakened.

Suddenly, the bells all rang out, and in the light of the waking sun, creeping from the horizon, like a tsunami, an avalanche of snow flooded across the land, on the air and into the sky,

It was much taller than the city walls and its pace, its speed, was terrifying.

Death was assured.

Borgian raced past the inn and only then realised that he had forgotten to wake Emi and Lasgot, it was too late now.

Then, without warning, the snow entered in, swallowing the city, everyone started running for their lives except those who were paralysed with fear or those who had been waiting for this, an excuse to die rather than direct suicide.

People headed to the other side of the city where they escaped through the south gate.

Borgian looked back at the inn as it was consumed by the snow, he was running with the others now, there was no way he could return back.

He muttered a prayer of good health to his friend who now resided in the Elysium.

There was a push for people to try and escape and the huge, colossal wave of ice and snow was so close now.

Borgian tried to move through the crowds but it was almost impossible, he started to shove, and a path seemed to almost magically open with the power of a little violence, he took a leap and he had escaped the city but that wasn't enough.

He ran a bit longer and could still feel the freeze of the snow on the back of his legs but at once, he was rid of it.

He had escaped and was greeted with the terrified faces of the surviving half of the city.

Nobody had expected this; the Malice of Snow had devoured Sesan and many lives were lost.

The city was full of snow, buried beneath the frigid danger.

Only the tallest towers could be seen, poking their heads from the mass of snow encapsulating the structures.

Children were crying, mothers mourning, fathers searching.

Whole families had been wiped from existence.

Sesan was no more and people were sent retreating as the weight of the snow finally crushed the structures of the tower's bottoms so that they exploded onto the ground, sending loose bricks, debris and shrapnel in all directions.

Borgian thought to himself, this was, all in truth, his fault, he had lost his friend and a whole city.

So many of its resident's lives destroyed.

He was a murderer.

By evening's coming, some people had already fled to other cities but many more, including Borgian, had remained, camping out in tents, waiting to see if there was a chance of their families coming back from the wreckage.

Borgian stayed there to help.

The guilt he felt was over encumbering.

Lamps lit the area and guided people to their temporary tent residences, Borgian found his own, he rested himself on a lion skin blanket and fell into a deep sleep.

The symbol on his hand lit up...

"HELP!" a blood-chilling shriek rang out into the cold morning air, "HELP ME!"

Borgian ran out of his tent to see many other people awake, yawning, stretching in the early hours.

The tent that the scream had emitted from was being approached.

"Stay back," Borgian warned some men herding around the tent, hoping to prove their bravery.

Borgian got out his sword, Slayer, and just as a pale blue-eyed man with greenish-blue skin overlapping his clearly rotting flesh and with drying blood around his mouth, appeared.

Borgian had seen one of these people before in a book, as an illustration, people diseased and mutated by a viral plague originating from the Malice of Snow.

The infected were known usually as 'The Disavowed' however in this one's case, due to not being an Elv, was a simple afflicted.

Borgian shoved Slayer into the thing's neck.

Borgian knew there was no point looking for survivors within.

Ulric appeared at the tent from out of nowhere, "This is enough, we need to take action, we need to get out of here."

Borgian nodded.

"Everyone!" Borgian called out, standing on a raised rock, "my name is Borgian Steel."

A few people tutted at this, knowing Borgian's previous disreputable occupation but apart from that, people were silent, too tired to object to him talking.

"There is a curse upon Askaria, the Malice of Snow, it can cause destruction and bloodshed as we've never seen before, and disease and I promise, more will happen, we must run and pray that the Edicryte will have mercy on us."

"How are we meant to trust you, bandit!" someone in the crowd shouted out.

"Because I trust him, he was the first person to take some sort of action against the curse, and to report it to me," Ulric stated, "so let him bloody speak."

"I promise you in the name of your pain and loss, I will find a way to stop this curse and I will bring you to safety, now, we must go to the Forelands, Mezal city is closest and I'm sure they will provide us with warm residence and good food, now, pack up and move."

The herds of people seemed to move at once, within half an hour, they were ready to depart.

Borgian lead them on.

He was going to keep his promise, he plunged Askaria into this mess and now he was going to pull it out.

Borgian noticed night falling as the moon appeared in the sky.

This faintly reminded Borgian of a biblical story he had once heard about how the moons were egg children of the goddess queen, Leirsi who was cursed never to make an immortal child with her husband, the god of the earth, Tersi.

Every time a full moon entered the sky, a child of Leirsi was born and when it disappeared, it died, and every time it returned, another was reborn in its place only to die again in an endless cycle.

Ulric also seemed to notice the falling night, "Borgian, we should stop, my people need rest."

"Of course, but not here, we're too far out at the border between the Forelands and the Benedoecs, this is a prime spot and a prime time for bandits to attack."

"Really, Borgian, you expect a few bandits to be able to take on this group of thousands of people? If they dared attack us, they'd be more stupid than a Dosvirian trader trying to haggle with a smithy from Raven's Breach," Ulric gave Borgian an annoyed look, Borgian could see Ulric had heavy bags under his eyes, his face was as pale as chalk.

Borgian noticed the idiocy of what he had just said about the bandits, having been one himself, he should've known, from experience, that bandits didn't attack such large groups.

"That's a good point," Borgian exclaimed stupidly, "we'll camp here for the night, but I would still feel safer in my bed if guards were to take shifts, against the beasts of the land."

Ulric nodded, "Yes," before telling his soldiers to report to the people that they could begin to settle down.

Everybody began to rebuild the tents, lay out the bearskin beds and light lamps around the area almost immediately.

Ulric drew in a breath and exhaled deeply, "Where do I go from here?"

"I don't know enough about my future to tell another man's."

"Thank you again, Borgian, I wouldn't have been able to get as many people out as I did, if not for you," Ulric gave Borgian a final nod of acknowledgement before retreating to his tent.

It was quiet for once, it was late night, everyone was probably asleep by now but Borgian was not.

He was worrying, stressing.

He was too tired to see his stress the last night.

He really didn't have an idea in which direction his life would go in.

He decided to step out of his tent for some fresh air, it was cool outside, the trees were alit in the glow of the lamps and the ultra-bright Askarian stars dancing above.

There was a light hooting from a not so far away owl.

The whole thing was beautiful.

Suddenly, a noise sounded, a branch cracking—Borgian wasn't the only thing here that didn't feel like sleeping.

He maintained caution, walking slowly forward, he could see something now, someone, someone climbing up onto a large jutting rock in the ground.

Borgian walked on, the figure was small, it couldn't be a Disavowed like he had originally feared.

The figure sat down on top of the rock.

Borgian leapt up carefully on the rock too, it was a child who sat on top, a young boy; he looked about six, with pale blue eyes and light ginger hair.

He looked bothered.

"Are you okay?" Borgian whispered so not to wake anyone up, he made the boy jump.

The boy stared at Borgian for a few seconds like he was trying to figure something out.

"I'm okay," was what the boy finally came out with, he went back to staring at the ground below.

"What are you doing out here? Shouldn't you be getting some rest?"

"Listening to the night, can you hear the owl too?"

"Yes, I can … where are your parents?"

"Gone, I lost them when it snowed."

"Do you know anyone around here?"

"No," the boy was looking up at the sky, "I'm afraid of being up in the sky, aren't you?"

Borgian looked up too, "Yes, yes I am."

"What's your name?" The boy asked inquisitively.

"Borgian, and your name?"

"Joric Barrol."

Borgian had heard of that name before, the Barrols were one of the great families of Sesan, Joric must have been the heir.

"Do you know who you are, young man?"

Joric shook his head ferociously.

"You are a Barrol, one of the great families of Sesan, you are destined for greatness, everything's going to be alright especially for someone like you."

The boy looked at Borgian and nodded, he then began to look up at the sky again.

Borgian stayed, sitting there for a while more, watching the stars and the moon as they disappeared behind eerie clouds.

"You're not going to be in the sky for a long time."

CHAPTER 7
FOR ALL REASONS

3 DAYS AFTER THE DESTRUCTION OF SESAN

"We have arrived," Borgian announced.

After three days of slow walking, they had made it.

Starving after they had exhausted their food source, they had finally reached the gates of Mezal city, and the walls of cold stone that didn't have to speak a word to state their superiority.

Now, Borgian had to hope for the pity of Clan Alok.

"Borgian, old friend, is that you," a cheerful voice rung out.

Mazdol Herginn came around the corner accompanied by his soldiers who bore the black bull and dagger on their red chest plates.

Borgian walked over to Mazdol and they thumped each other's backs in greeting, they had been good friends since Borgian had once saved Mazdol from the bandit king, Utalar Ironfist.

"It's been too long," Borgian exclaimed.

"It has, say, when did you become lord of all these people."

"In Sesan's current state, I wouldn't want to lord over it, Lord Ulric is following behind, most likely mourning with his people," Borgian took a breather, "Mazdol, the Malice of Snow has awakened."

Mazdol glanced at the half of the people of Sesan that had survived.

"These people are from Sesan? And the Malice of Snow, are you sure? I've only heard of it in legend."

"You'd know if I was lying, I wouldn't have dragged half a city of people into the wilds of the Forelands to starve, if such chaos hadn't occurred," Borgian replied grimly.

Borgian continued, "And why are you here Mazdol, outside your greatest enemy's city."

Mazdol suddenly returned to his usual irritated face, "Clan Alok stole my entranced daughter, I am going to try and bring her back the peaceful way, otherwise..."

Mazdol signalled at his soldiers who stood to attention.

"It's still a small amount of protection for you, isn't it?" Borgian looked upon Mazdol's meek group of just over fifty soldiers.

"Well, I didn't want Zensi to think I was attacking, this is enough just to make sure I get what's mine."

Borgian was confused, he's never seen this side of Mazdol that didn't want to full-on cripple everything in his path so that he could get his way.

"Then may we go in and come back out with what we both seek now."

The two approached the great doors, the guards seemed understandably hesitant to let Mazdol in, "Mazdol, I'm afraid you're not allowed past these gates, didn't you know that?" one of the guards sniggered.

"He'll be good, he just came to claim his property," Borgian reasoned.

"And why are you here, you don't look like the usual Herginn idiot," the soldier looked Borgian up and down, trying to identify him.

"Sesan, the Malice of Snow struck."

The guard pulled a long face, looking down the line of Sesan's previous citizens.

"You're joking?" the soldier gave Borgian a stern look.

"Does that line of people behind me, look like they're joking?" Borgian inquired.

The guard gave the line of people another look before concluding: "Go on in then."

"And Mazdol?" Borgian queried.

The guard gave a slight nod, "Fine, but don't tell Zensi I let him in," the soldier then quickly added, "and his men will have to stay here."

Mazdol gave a returned nod and made his soldiers stay behind.

They entered in, straight through the first narrow street and up to the largest house in the city, Mazdol and Borgian went.

The citizens of Sesan, Ulric and Mazdol's guards were left behind the gate to wait anxiously and patiently.

The large spruce doors of the longhouse were opened and Zensi stood up at once, her guards engaged.

They circled Mazdol and angled their spears at his throat.

"I would like my daughter please," Mazdol intoned sarcastically whilst pushing one of the soldier's spears threatening his neck, downwards, "this isn't the warm welcome I was expecting."

Zensi smiled at this sight, she went over and reassigned the soldier's spear to Mazdol's neck again.

"I'll consider it if you'd kindly shut up, it was foolish for you to come here, I could kill you now if I wanted to."

She spotted Borgian, "And why are you here, one of Mazdol's guards?"

"No, my counte—"

"Don't call her that, she's got to earn the title first," Mazdol countered.

"Shut up Herginn, and you, please continue," Zensi beckoned to Borgian.

"It was at Sesan, the Malice of Snow, it destroyed everything, only half of the city including Lord Ulric survived, they wait outside your walls."

Zensi exchanged a fearful glance with Georlia—her prophecy had taken form faster than expected.

"I will be able to grant Sesan's people its salvation and will alert the other city leaders of this danger, a council will be held, the leaders of Askaria will be called," Zensi stopped, glancing at Herginn for a moment.

"And my daughter?"

"Sorry, what daughter? Mazdol," Zensi decided she was going to play with him.

"Let's not play childish games Zensi, bring me my daughter," Mazdol looked to the soldiers who glared at him, unimpressed.

"Okay, but only on one condition."

"Name it," Mazdol's eyes locked on Zensi unhappily.

"A temporary truce, no attacks on enemy land," Zensi extended a hand, Mazdol shook it impatiently and un-joyfully, "once this is all over, if we can end it, then things will go back to normal. And keep your daughter away from my son."

"Someone, go get his daughter, please," Zensi turned towards Borgian, "and, you, your name?"

"Borgian Steel"

Zensi smirked, "The ex-bandit, how ironic for you to be the one responsible for shepherding a city, or half a city," Zensi turned to Mazdol, remembering he was there, "you can leave now."

The spears of the soldiers were lowered and Mazdol nodded begrudgingly.

"Thank you, Countess," Borgian obliged, Mazdol also muttered something under his breath as he saw his daughter arrive through a door.

They left the city and Lord Ulric awaited the news, "What happened? Can my people take refuge?"

Borgian replied, "Yes and word has been sent to the great cities, a council is to be held."

"Good, I can only stress for the future of my people now and must ensure their wellbeing," Ulric turned to leave.

"I hope you find some rest in your life."

Ulric turned back around to face Borgian.

"Until this mayhem passes, my people are completely safe, and Zensi wears the First Crown on her head, I'll never rest, Borgian.

CHAPTER 8
ELVEN BLOOD

Zensi Alok spoke to Mazdol Herginn, Ulric Crewe and Borgian Steel about the success.

"Most lords and Countesses have decided to attend the meeting."

"Most, I'm guessing its Clan Gordanyes of Sairoh, Clan Benortitein of Hernight and..."

"Clan Sahjan of Fallanstar that aren't coming," Zensi finished Mazdol's sentence.

"We're probably better off without the insufferable 'High Lord Aminucilie Sahjan of the Askarian Elves' and without the rest of them, aren't we?" Mazdol put forth his opinion.

"No, we are not, Aminucilie has a great influence on this land, perhaps more powerful than ours, we need him."

"Maybe I could help here," Lord Ulric placed, "I knew Aminucilie from childhood, our fathers were friends."

"Partnered snobs from an early age, eh," Mazdol humoured himself, everyone ignored him.

"That would be helpful," Borgian remarked at Ulric.

"Set up a carriage, Fallanstar isn't too far away, a carriage should take you there directly, and Borgian, you should accompany Ulric, he's likely to need some protection on the roads."

Zensi clapped her hands and a trio of guards ran through to obey her orders.

By noon, the carriage was set, and the sun was stark middle in the sky, lighting the tents which resided outside the city walls and gave temporary residence to the people of Sesan.

At the carriage, two guards stood representing clans: Crewe and Herginn.

Mazdol arrived—dressed in skins and furs, overdressed, you could say.

He could have been mistaken for a bear if he was on all fours and had more hair than just his brown, struck with grey, stubble and fading hazel hair.

"I'm coming, I'm sure Zensi would prefer me to go and I will, even if I hate to make her feel comfortable," Mazdol told.

The carriage was off through the damp Foreland forests, following the crumbling Forgemaster's Path.

The carriage jolted on every bump of rigid stone, making the ride extremely uncomfortable.

"Is that it?" Ulric asked, taking sight of the shimmering, golden, marble towers decorating the city front.

"I've only ever seen the prison walls of this place, but I'd hazard a guess that's the city," Borgian voiced.

The city was a blinding collection of amazing architecture, rimmed with diamonds and rubies reflecting the great sun, the rest of the city was a pure, rich moon-white.

The houses seemed to be suspended by great willows, the biggest one of all had a set of stairs which lead out of the city walls and replaced the gate which would be seen at any other city.

The three men ascended the steps and were met with the very tall, pale-skinned and exquisitely grey-eyed elves who looked the men down and sniggered in their own language, making a joke that neither Mazdol, Borgian or Ulric could translate.

Borgian used what small knowledge of elven speech he had, to attain understanding with the elven soldiers who eventually let the trio in, opening the heavy doors of the house with surprising grace.

Inside was the type of majesty that could bring men down to their knees, crying in front of—the glory and beauty illuminated by the light of the sun.

"Ulric, what are you doing here?" the voice was silk and as soft as sin.

It came from a tall man with large, pointed ears, blond hair and wearing a white robe with silver lining and a sapphire encrusted torso.

"Yes, Aminucilie, I am here to ask you exactly why you refuse to help us destroy the curse that will surely destroy you or, with you not attending, perhaps others will be annoyed enough to kill you because of your ignorance," Ulric expressed, "you can literally see the very ruins of Sesan from your balcony, half of the Benedoecs has been decimated by the snow, why do you refuse to join us?."

"In my city, never threaten me, I have my reasons, I do not trust it, an alliance established mainly by two feuding alliances, I don't see any reason to attend a meeting constructed in a way worse than a bastard child's construction of a meeting when born as a half-breed," Aminucilie finished.

Ulric was furious now and had risen to meet Aminucilie's gaze with angry eyes.

"I have seen my whole city crumble, watched my people bleed to death with ice through their chests, lose their limbs to the cold, I have nothing," Ulric tried to keep in tears.

Borgian noticed Aminucilie's guards engage slightly.

"And yet two clans are willing to put their feud aside to give my people and the whole civilisation of Askaria a chance to survive and to help destroy the curse which I have seen with my eyes, that cry out in the hope that the hundreds of people; mothers, fathers, children, and those children stained red with inevitable death, I hope that in death, they can live the life they never got to live in this world and that they will forgive me for not saving them," Ulric couldn't contain himself, he shouted out in rage and with tears in his eyes, "I trust the people that have given sanctuary to what remains of my people, so how about you lock up your stupidity and insolence and trust them too!"

Aminucilie was obviously shocked but tried not to show it, nobody had ever stood up to him like that, Ulric was the person who he least expected to do so.

Ulric had seen much but he was still strong.

Aminucilie was in awe and his face was red with embarrassment, he struggled for words and in the end, simply said, "Walk with me."

He beckoned Ulric to follow him.

They both walked out into the gardens, where Aminucilie spoke.

"How can you possibly expect me to trust Mazdol and the intentions of everyone else, don't be mad, this is all just another way for him to gain a hold on Zensi."

"You don't need to trust Mazdol, you just need to trust me, please, just for an old friend, Zensi knows what she's doing, we just need your help," Ulric pleaded.

There was silence and even the birds in the palace gardens had gone quiet.

Aminucilie refused to reply.

Ulric was left to one last resource, he hated to do this but he knew it was the only way.

"Leyla's in The Eye and The Mouth, she doesn't know what's happened, I haven't told her yet."

"Leyla's with the Missionaries?" Aminucilie replied in surprise.

"A trade agreement," Ulric explained, "believe it or not, the Missionaries were where Sesan attained all its wealth from. We got a large portion of all they owned because no-one else was going to trade with them.."

"And for good reason," Aminucilie spoke, clutching his arm.

"They were seen in Mezal last, their grip on Askaria is increasing, if the Malice of Snow kills us all, they'll start moving in on whatever's left, including you and everyone like you."

"I see what you're doing," Aminucilie realised, "I suggest you stop."

Aminucilie tried to make his way back to the palace and as he did, Ulric spoke.

"If you won't do it for me, do it for him and everyone else like you."

Aminucilie turned around fast and walked up to Ulric.

Ulric braced himself but Aminucilie simply hugged him.

"It's been too long, I wish we could go back to when we were children, before Mazdol and Zensi started this mess, before the Missionaries entered Askaria, before they took him."

"We can only rebuild from the rubble now, but only if there's still something left to repurpose," Ulric paused, "will you join me?"

"What happened?" Borgian asked.

"He came around."

CHAPTER 9
THE SNOW-BORN COUNCIL

They assembled in torchlight, in a cold stone room at the back of Mezal's oldest building, the prison.

They were all sat around the table, all but Borgian, who stood perched against a wall, silent.

The room was filled with the sound of lords and countesses muttering, their voices intertwined and echoed eerily around the dungeon.

They fell quiet as Zensi began.

"We are here assembled as the Snow-Born Council to discuss a danger that will bring death quicker than our blades on the field, as many of you are probably aware, a great curse known as the Malice of Snow sweeps the land, it has been dormant for thousands of years but its back, we are here to discuss how we can stop it, and what we know of it."

She took a breath, inhaling the cold air that seeped through the many crevices in the dungeon bricks.

She breathed out.

"Before it's too late..."

A long silence followed, and a small amount of whispering broke out among the lords, it didn't sound related to the subject and as the whispering turned into full-on conversations, Borgian looked to Zensi just before she snapped.

She stood up, slammed her fist down on the old, hard wooden table and shouted, "Do you not understand the situation, if you don't think this is important then look to your rights and lefts, you will find that the most powerful men and women in all of Askaria lie to every side of you, what does that mean to you? Do you believe I'd invite you all here on a less threatening matter?" she brought her fist back to her side, Borgian could see it was covered with splinters and coated in blood, "maybe you all just simply do not care."

She returned to her seated position where she began to remove the splinters out from her hand's flesh, under the table.

Another long silence followed.

And then there came a timid voice.

A lord called Arin Sheal, son of the leader of the western city of Westgard, was the owner of this voice.

"When I was young, I was told a story about the Malice of Snow, it was said to have wiped out an entire race, the White Elves, any information would be where they died, Bolgron Island."

"Where did yeh learn tha'?" Lord Bogstot Clairn, a clearly overweight man with a large black beard and a scent of beer, asked with amusement.

Borgian wondered if a lord as young as Arin would know what Bogstot was hinting at.

"Not as a child being fed milk," Arin Sheal told Bogstot in a stone-cold tone.

Hmm, he did know.

Most were told stories when 'receiving' their milk.

Bogstot gave a hearty laugh, "Good, Good."

"Please be serious Bogstot," Zensi called from across the table they were sitting at.

"Hmm, hmm, so how do yeh 'spect to get to Bolgron Island?" Bogstot asked.

"With ships," informed Lord Terrowin Ceize, a blackish-purple skinned member of the reptilian race of Cecropians, in a matter-of-fact tone.

"Yeah, I'm aware of tha', snake man," Bogstot voiced.

"I'm sorry, then why did you ask, common man?" Terrowin replied with distaste and sarcasm, "I'd happily sail down the lake, one of my ships for the cause."

"I would greatly appreciate that, thank you, but who would go, if I have been informed well, a plague comes spread from the curse and could still be active on Bolgron."

"I would not worry, my queen," Borgian saw Mazdol flinch out of the corner of his eye at the mention of the word, 'queen', "a friend of mine has traversed Bolgron Island before, as far as I have been told, the disease has killed off all of its hosts, no hosts, no disease, although saying that, he was only on the island for two hours and above ground," Borgian announced and reassured.

"Someone went to Bolgron," Mazdol exclaimed, surprised, "why..."

"He went looking for treasure," were the only words to leave Borgian's mouth.

Mazdol may have said something else but was too slow, someone else decided it was their turn to speak.

"Perhaps I could help, I've had my fair share of adventuring, my husband's city, Drumdallg, doesn't offer much in entertainment in the way of women, and alcohol is only for men so it's the outer lands—The Longlands—that are my source of entertainment," spoke the beautiful Countess Elisia, married to Lord Bogstot.

"So Elisia and Borgian, would you mind, I understand it is a lot to ask, attending to this?" Zensi looked to Borgian for an answer.

"It poses no problem in my way."

"And that is all?" Bogstot asked, eyeing his wife with an anxious uncertainty.

Zensi tutted, "Yes, that is all."

"Not quite," Mazdol put in, "who is to lead the Snow-Born Council, all factions require a leader, as told in the ancient 72 Laws of Arch King Vanible Herginn."

"You invite us to a council of freeing Askaria from a curse and only to try and bind us in your chains, another curse, we are our own leaders until the next Arch King ... or Queen," Aminucilie expressed his support to Zensi by giving her a slight nod.

"What the elf said, we'r our own leaders," Lord Bogstot mumbled, leaking ale, that he had somehow got hold of, down his beard.

"And for your notes, Mazdol, no one leads this council, the laws of a dead Herginn king should be forgotten or at least exposed for what they are, the commands of a paranoid, weak man, a man like you, Mazdol," Zensi smugly grinned at Mazdol.

Mazdol stood up, "Don't you talk about weak, in case everyone in this room has forgotten, I drove a blade through your father's back and you just cowered in the shadows, watching."

Zensi's face seemed to turn a beetroot colour, Mazdol had made a mistake.

And before anyone could predict what was about to happen next, Zensi unsheathed an expertly crafted throwing knife from under her elegant, green dress and aimed it just left of Mazdol's head, it hit well and true and dug deep into the wooden board laid against the wall behind him.

"You want to know what I was doing in the shadows, Herginn," she gave him a venomous glare, "I was observing the way in which I'd kill you, the same way you killed my father, I had a child with me then, I'm not willing to sacrifice children, something I'm sure you'd do."

Mazdol turned to look behind himself at the knife, before standing up and removing it from its wooden resting place.

He pointed with the knife at various people in the room and gave them a description as he did.

Bogstot: "A perpetual drunk,", Arin: "A person too young to understand politics,", Terrowin and Aminucilie: "Non-humans with no rights to the titles of lords," and finally Zensi: "A disgusting, ignorant would-be-usurper with a suicidal mind."

Borgian had not been given a tag, thankfully.

Mazdol then scrunched up his face, "I will be leaving now."

Zensi shook her head, "If it wasn't for this new threat to Askaria, that knife would have penetrated your skull and you would be dead," Zensi turned away and proceeded to walk out the room, "I pity you."

Mazdol went silent, annoyed, he threw the knife to the ground and stormed off.

The rest of the lords remained seated.

They were in shock.

Borgian decided now would be a good time to tell the council how the Malice of Snow became.

By his doing.

"It's time I told you all something, the reason why I stand here amongst you lords and countesses."

That night, he told them all about how he caused the curse to come again.

Some would leave honouring him for his determination to end wars, others would leave, disgusted, because of his greed...

CHAPTER 10
A DELAYED DEPARTURE

Borgian was pleasantly awakened in the morning to the sound of birds tweeting and the gentle warmth of the rays of sunlight creeping through the windows of the tower he had been sleeping in, his first thoughts for the morning were to thank Zensi for her hospitality towards the previous citizens of Sesan, and to inform her of his upcoming departure to Bolgron Island.

He and Elisia Clairn were to meet with the captain of the ship and to go aboard the ship itself, which would be arriving at the Rylus, a riverbank on the Lake Hillbridge—famous for its black sands.

The tower he currently resided in was known as the Forering Tower, it was a tower directly centred in a ring of stone wall guarding the front of the city and needing to be gone through if someone wanted access to the rest of the city.

It was a circle, a ring of wall that came before everything else, hence the name: Forering.

The tower had three large rooms, three large fireplaces, three large windows and one small barrack, the more important barracks were within the city, where Zensi currently resided, most likely in her, more than anything fortress-like, long hall named the Palace Hall.

That was Borgian's destination.

He descended a tiny, steep staircase within the tower and came straight to the exit door, Borgian opened it out into the cold morning air of the city, it smelled of smoke.

This reminded Borgian of his last quest with Lasgot, the quest that would ultimately lead to his friend's death.

Borgian remembered the heavy smoke there.

And the rattling sound that the corrupt elv made...

When Borgian had made his way into the city, he was greeted with a sight more pleasant than that of one he had once received in Talgrin city.

In Mezal city, they had a sewage system which in Talgrin city, was absent.

In Talgrin city, the streets were lined with the faeces of people, dogs, horses—all manner of things—in Mezal however, where Borgian stood now, the streets were clean.

Borgian acknowledged the tall, towering stone buildings that stood around him, scattered along the sides of the carriage path and the smoke that rose, like grey fog, from their chimneys, causing a cloud of smog to develop over the city.

At this time of day, the path seemed to be devoid of both horse, rider and carriage and the paths on the sides were relatively unpopulated apart from two well-dressed women who Borgian gave a nod, each, to.

Borgian suspected the lack of people was due to the earliness of the morning.

He started to doubt Zensi would be awake at this time but nevertheless; he continued up to the palace.

The way to the palace was boring from then on, peaceful, yes, but boring.

Borgian would have given anything for some company at this moment, which was unusual for him.

He started to consider that the loss of his friend had begun to, more thoroughly, kick in.

He would have given even more now, to have some company, now that he was starting to think of his dead friend...

Suddenly, at that moment, he caught sight of a group of grey-robed priests led by a white-robed man, wearing a silver mask and a bishop hat.

Borgian recognised them as the foreign group of priests following the religion, following the three gods known as the Trilords; Desarorn, the father of dragons; Bersiryd, the father of men; and Eliwyn, the father of mer.

The collective name for them was Missionaries, their reason for being in Askaria was to try and return and re-baptise Clan Benortitein of the Cold, under the Trilord religion that they once used to believe in, a long time ago.

They had settled outside of the city of Hernight where Clan Benortitein ruled the Cold from.

It was known that the Benortiteins had continued to reject the Missionaries and the Trilords alike.

What they were doing in Mezal city was beyond Borgian and as he passed by them, he received some insight into the reason they were there.

The first piece of information was from one of the minor priest's whisperings to the bishop.

"Another failure, are we to believe the whole of Askaria are to turn their backs on the Trilords, their original gods?"

"You know little, Harold, only half of the Askarian Clans were subject to the rules of the Trilords that they followed, those like Clan Alok and Clan Herginn have never followed our gods, I was expecting Zensi's decline today," the bishop told coolly.

"And, Bishop Visur, what do you expect for the rest of Askaria."

"Not much, the clans only ever followed the Trilords when Clan Benortitein did, hopefully when Benortitein return to their rightful rulers, so will all."

"And if they don't? If the Benortiteins never give in?"

"Then they can expect war, the Missionaries are more powerful than ever before, our holy islands of The Eye and The Mouth are more than ready to fight," Bishop Visur finished before turning around, eyeing his group and catching sight of Borgian, who quickly continued walking towards the palace.

"We are done here."

The Missionaries continued down the road leading back to the Forering.

War, Borgian thought, wasn't there already enough of it?

As Borgian finally entered the palace, gained recognition from the guards and the gates opened unto him, he pondered on what he had just heard.

There were too many wars going on for Borgian's liking; there was the War of the Crown between Zensi and Mazdol although it had been halted, the upcoming Battle of Winter, as Borgian had heard it called before, when the Malice of Snow unleashed its army and now, a possible new holy war.

Then there was the war going on in Borgian's head, the thought that he had caused one of these wars to soon unfold, had caused a city and thousands of people to be destroyed and had caused his friend to die.

More crime than he had committed during his entire life of banditry.

When Borgian had passed into the throne room, a soldier came up to him and announced, "Queen Zensi lies in the private infirmary."

"And that is where?" Borgian asked, feeling slightly dumb.

"Follow me," the soldier commanded, trying not to sound irritated.

Borgian did follow him, down a dark, dimly lit corridor and an arrangement of stairs, another corridor and then in, through a door.

"Queen Zensi," the soldier pounded his chest with honour before leaving Borgian with Zensi.

The door closed behind the soldier and in a glance of the room, Borgian looked upon an elderly man, that reminded Borgian of a mouse, as he removed the huge splinters, that Zensi had received from pounding the table yesterday, with a pair of tweezers.

When he was done with the removing in one site, he'd place the splinters in a bowl of, red from blood, water and apply a small amount of grey cream to a place on Zensi's hand.

"I won't be long, after this, we can head down to the stables," Zensi told.

"Yes, I came to thank you for the council yesterday and the hospitality you have shown to Sesan."

"Of course, I hope to be able to escort some of Sesan's people over to Lakewell soon, Lord Terrowin informs me has a number of empty houses available."

"That is good news," Borgian said, "unlike some I have heard today."

"Hmm?" Zensi edged him on.

"Missionaries."

Zensi grimaced "When I heard they had landed in Askaria, I hoped they would stay in Hernight but of late, sadly, many of my hopes have not been fulfilled," Zensi sighed, "rude, insignificant bastards, I hope that should be the last I see of them," she sighed again, "I'll have drunk myself sick on ale before the day's out, stress is slowly taking its toll on me."

"And so, I shouldn't tell you that if Clan Benortitein doesn't accept the Trilordic religion, that the Missionaries plan to wage war on Askaria."

Zensi put her face in her hands for a few seconds.

"Mazdol is already at the Rylus, it seems almost funny to say, that now, he's one of the least of my problems."

"All done," the man nursing to her hand announced before exiting the room.

"Good thing the man's deaf," Zensi whispered as if the man could hear her outside the room, "there are already too many rumours spreading around at that moment."

Borgian hadn't even considered blurting all this news out in front of the doctor.

"I suppose we best get down to the ship then."

Zensi nodded, "Let's go."

The horses seemed to sink into the mud as the two went along.

"I feel sorry for Elisia, she's probably already at the Rylus with Mazdol, talking about the fact he called her husband a perpetual drunk," Zensi voiced.

"I feel sorry for her because she is married to a perpetual drunk."

Zensi gave a short laugh.

There was silence, and then.

"Borgian, I wonder, have you ever felt like you're losing and winning at the same?"

"I'm sorry, I don't quite understand you," Borgian waited for Zensi to rephrase the question.

"Well, an example of winning and losing could be like the fact I'm winning because pretty much all clans support me however I'm also losing because none would fight against Mazdol, out of fear."

"And yet most of them, face to face with Mazdol, insulted him in the council yesterday," Borgian remembered.

"Yes, yes, they did," Zensi thought aloud, "I think the problem is that they can't see past the fact that Mazdol's huge army of trained soldier and bandit men, supplied by the bandit queen, Jerilla, is too big for me to take on. They don't see that if all my supporting clans united with me, that we would be unstoppable."

"It's always hard for men to see the future when the present is so much closer," Borgian told her as they both came into sight of a wooden sign with the words: Lake Hillbridge, carved into it.

"Getting closer now. How much further, driver!" Zensi shouted out to get the driver's attention over the sound of the rocking carriage.

"Not much further now, a journey through the valley, pick up your friends, and we should be by the water's side."

"Good."

"Which valley?" Borgian wondered aloud.

"The Valley of Slaa, the most rural of all places in Askaria, fields as far as the eyes can see, it's also the only unclaimed piece of land, by a clan, in this land," Zensi told.

"A great place for bandits," Borgian muttered.

"Depends what route you take," Zensi looked at Borgian meaningfully.

"And your friends? Who are they?" Borgian looked at her meaningfully, this time.

"One is a Dosvirian warrior by the name of Thalt, son of the king of Dosviri, he used to fight in the Black Arena and won as high champion, he was then picked up as commander of the Imperial Elite, sworn to Emperor Calclius, lately he has retired, but not quite, obviously."

"A man with strength and a story, good, and the other."

"The other," Zensi told, "is a young man called Howers, a man of mental strength with a knack for unravelling ancient mysteries, he first gained fame for discovering the burial place of Arch King Massus."

"Sounds like a good pair of people," Borgian opinionated happily.

"Yes."

Soon enough, through the trees surrounding the paths, rays of sun began to peek their tongues through the trees overhead and lick the ground below.

Borgian stared out into the illuminated valley, sparsely filled with quaint cottages and tall, oak trees and covered over with ponds and sparkling rivers.

"It's the only unspoilt piece of land in the whole continent, the only place where no one has a right to, and if Mazdol dared say anything of taking it over, I'd come murder him in his own hall even if I risked dying myself, Slaa is the most important of all places here," Zensi stated.

Suddenly, then, a deer ran in front of the carriage, it was a large, magnificent beast and was gone within a couple of seconds.

"That was close," Borgian exclaimed, trying to catch sight of it in the area it had run off to.

"An abundance of wildlife here, if anyone is caught hunting in this area, it's not a law, but if they're brought to me, I'll sentence them to the same fate as the poor creature they killed."

"You'd kill them?" Borgian exclaimed, surprised.

"Well, they'd be hunted, they'd be brought back here, allowed to run, and then chased by my bowmen. They'd be shot down," Zensi smiled, "a just fate for such evil men, one that should be carried out in all worlds alike."

"And hunters outside of Slaa, what about them?"

"Well, if they are known to my court and hunting for food, and—Zensi put empathises on the 'and'—"most definitely hunting outside of Slaa, their purpose may be considered."

"We have arrived," the driver announced.

In front of them was a small tower.

"Welcome to the Alok Estate Tower, Borgian, my friends should be in here."

"What exactly is this?" Borgian asked.

"It was a project established a while ago, it keeps hunters in check, Mazdol away and gives me some home away from home, one day, when this war is behind me, I intend to make this place into a self-sustaining farming village," Zensi looked up the wooden tower, "an interesting dream, I suppose."

Zensi put a key into the lock and opened the door.

What came before Borgian's eyes was a man more silver beard than face with his twin daggers in his hands, and behind that was another man with darkened blonde features and a small knife in his right hand.

As soon as the men saw Zensi, however, they immediately put their weapons away.

"Queen Zensi," The two spoke together, "shall we get going?"

The sand was black there like Borgian had heard but the riverbank was larger than he had imagined, the Rylus seemed to take up both sides of the lake and into the distance, it went.

Borgian and Elisia were already gathered on the beach with both, five soldiers each, looking both as irritated as each other.

When they saw Borgian and Zensi, their faces lit up slightly, for Mazdol, more Borgian than Zensi.

"You took your precious time," Mazdol exclaimed as he came over to greet Borgian.

Borgian saw Elisia go over to Zensi and heard her saying something about Mazdol, along the lines of him being a complete twat.

After they were all done greeting each other, Thalt and Howers introduced themselves to the group and after some time had passed and conversations that felt like they had happened days ago sank into silence, people began to wonder where the ship was.

"It should have been here by now," Mazdol was the first to show his annoyance, "has the snake man forgotten."

Elisia gave a laugh, "You're using the words of my husband who you called a perpetual drunk."

Mazdol ignored her.

Borgian thought that he probably knew she was right.

Zensi was the second to break, "Where the hell are they, this is ridiculous!" she huffed, "a few more minutes and I'm headed back to the estate, I'll stay there for the bloody night!"

Zensi looked at the two men, Thalt and Howers, "I'm sorry for wasting your time, I understand how far you had to travel to get here, please feel free to any inn you wish in Mezal and I'll pay for your fayres back."

Suddenly, at that moment, the vast hull of a ship came around the corner.

"Oh, thank the gods!" Zensi shouted out in relief.

Borgian wasn't sure how to feel, he would have been okay to stay in Askaria in all honesty and now, there was no turning back.

As the party of people on the beach began to clap in the arrival of the ship, the sound of a horn rang through the air.

Unusual.

The next thing to make Borgian worry was as the ship neared the Rylus, he spotted a flag showing three towers on it, and it wasn't the flag of Lakewell, Borgian knew exactly what the flag was of, and fear filled him.

"RUN!" Borgian shouted just as a rain of burning arrows broke the sky.

Zensi and Mazdol were the first to run followed by Thalt.

Borgian quickly caught sight of Elisia and Howers, they were paralysed and as the arrows began to fall, Borgian had to make a quick decision.

He jumped.

He found himself on Elisia and quickly rolled her over as the arrows hit the ground...

Zensi, Mazdol and Thalt had made it over a hidden ridge.

Borgian whispered in Elisia's ear, "Okay, when I say, you're going to run to that ridge, alright, don't stop."

Elisia nodded.

Borgian began a countdown, "Three, two, one..."

Borgian quickly jumped up.

"NOW!"

Elisia ran, she saw the corpses of her soldiers and the body of Howers on the floor, arrows sticking out of his heart.

More arrows rained and as Elisia made it to the ridge, she turned around quickly to see one of the arrows pierce Borgian's leg.

He fell.

"Are you okay," Zensi asked Elisia when she was over the ridge.

"Yes, I'm fine."

Over the ridge, they watched as Borgian was picked up by a group of semi-armoured people and hauled onto the ship.

"We need to get back out there," Mazdol whispered.

"You must be kidding me, Mazdol, how stupid are you, we need backup."

"Zensi, I'm sorry to tell you this but we are not going to get backup out here," Thalt said as he began to get undressed, "in situations like this, you have to take things up upon yourself."

When he was only in his undergarment, he explained his plan.

"They'll see us coming on land, but not if we're underwater, I intend to go around the ship, into the water and break the man free," Thalt looked at the rest of the group who stood in silence, "no objections, good."

Zensi looked as if she wanted to say something but the words didn't form in her mouth.

"So, when do you intend to go?" Mazdol asked rather rudely.

"Now," Thalt whispered, "when the ship is safe, I will fire a flaming arrow beyond this ridge," he nodded and then he was off.

"He realises that we're also beyond the ridge, right?" Elisia looked at Zensi and Mazdol.

"He's Dosvirian, I doubt it even crossed his foreign mind."

Night had fallen by the time Thalt had reached the backside of the ship.

He was drenched and cold, but he had been in worse positions.

He hauled himself up onto the deck of the ship to peep over and was met with a row of bandits patrolling the ship, there were about six, this would be easy.

Thalt lowered himself down, then he whistled and what he expected to happen, successfully took place.

A couple of the patrol came to the edge of the ship and were immediately struck in the head by Thalt, with knives in his hands.

He used the knives in the skulls of the bandit's heads to support himself up on the ship.

When he had mounted the vessel, he proceeded to kill the rest of the unaware bandits.

He stabbed his knives through backs, the backs of heads and the backs of legs.

The bandits had slow minds.

Slow reactions.

Thalt had quick hands...

And a quick mind.

When Thalt had finished off the patrol team, he took one of the bows from the deck, lit an arrow in a barrel of tar, and fired it beyond the ridge.

The ship would be safe before they got here, that was without a doubt.

At that moment, Thalt heard creaking floorboards, he quickly turned around just in time to see a bandit raise his knife.

Thalt swiftly dodged, drew another arrow in his newly acquired bow, and shot.

The arrow found it's mark in the bandit's head—even the quick-minded ones were no match.

"Morons," Thalt exclaimed as he moved towards the lower deck entrance.

The door was kicked open, Thalt threw a knife almost as soon as he had entered.

He abandoned the bow and returned to his loyal twin daggers.

Sticking people in their hearts, and sometimes their eyes.

"Wow, you're a clumsy one, aren't you," Thalt directed his mock towards a bandit who almost tripped on his way towards him.

They clashed swords.

"And yet you're the first man who hasn't died in the first second of meeting me on this ship," Thalt announced before headbutting the man, and allowing him to fall to the floor.

Thalt proceeded to ram the man against the wall of the ship and holding him there when the bandit had hoped to stand up.

"So, where's ya captive?" Thalt asked the man begrudgingly.

"Who? Borgian?"

"Who else do you bloody think I'm talking about?"

"He's on the captains' deck, with the rest of them."

"Them?"

"All the other shame bringing Tanlor bandits who thought they could just leave."

"You can't say much about shame, you just told me where your captives are."

The bandit pulled an annoyed face before Thalt put a sword from the floor, through the bandit's mouth.

Blood dribbled from the bandit like saliva from an absent baby.

Thalt quickly continued, descending a set of wooden stairs going downwards and finding himself in a dingy, darker part of the ship.

In the little torchlight illuminating the room, Thalt could make out the silhouettes of around ten people, he detached a torch from its holder and scanned the faces of these people, looking for Borgian's.

Thalt was unhappy to find that the majority of those before him, were dead.

He found only one alive, sleeping, maybe, Thalt thought, before he came across Borgian.

He breathed a sigh of relief.

Although he had never properly got acquainted with this man, he had become part of the job that would earn Thalt the promised amount of money from Zensi to re-establish his lost cause.

Borgian's death would be the ultimate deal-breaker, and thankfully Borgian was alive.

"Borgian."

"Thalt," Borgian inclined his head slightly to look at him.

"I'm going to get you out of here," Thalt assured him as he readied his knife to cut the rope bindings.

Dread then sunk its hooks into Thalt as he came to the realisation that his knife wouldn't be able to break the bindings because the bindings were lock and key, platinum chains.

"Key?" Where is it?"

Thalt shook Borgian as he started to look like he was about to drop off.

"Borgian!" Thalt whisper shouted.

Borgian remained silent.

His eyes closed.

Thalt stood up.

He moved to the other side of the room, passing back to the man he thought was just sleeping before.

He shook him, he woke immediately.

"I can help you, where's the key?"

Thalt waited for an answer but received none.

The man's face was page-white and seemed almost emotionless.

Maybe he had something wrong with him.

Maybe he was deaf.

The silence began to annoy Thalt but was necessary for him to almost save himself.

Thalt began to hear quiet footsteps as he crouched down on the floor.

The bound man's eyes suddenly enlarged with fear.

Thalt quickly turned around.

A figure stood poised to kill.

The scimitar held in the figure's hand plunged downwards but dropped to the floor instead of cutting into flesh.

Thalt was sprayed with a warm liquid over his bare skin.

Thalt tasted blood on his lips, metallic on his tongue.

A feminine figure stood behind the would-be-killer's kneeled body.

Thalt recognised the woman, Elisia.

She looked shocked at herself.

"Thank you very much," Thalt said to the dark shadow.

The figure nodded before a small silver item was passed to Thalt, the key.

Thalt, with haste, unlocked Borgian's chains, he then slung him over his shoulder.

"Let's get to the deck."

They moved forwards, upwards.

They were greeted with the metallic smell of blood from the previously killed dead, the air filled with the scent of wet pines and the rain that poured down from the sky, cold and unwelcoming.

"Great weather for sailing," Thalt exclaimed sarcastically.

On the shore, through the fog and the darkness of the night, could Zensi and Mazdol be seen, with soldiers holding torches, illuminating the night with an orange glow.

Zensi did not wave but gave them a nod.

Mazdol simply stood before departing with his soldiers behind him.

Thalt lay Borgian down on the floor of the deck.

Elisia watched with bated breath, for him to take the wheel.

A magpie landed directly in front of her and opened its beak to show many rows of sharp, black teeth.

Elisia jumped back in shock.

"Did you see that!" She directed her voice towards Thalt.

"See what?" Thalt jumped up from nursing Borgian and allowed his eyes to wander and find what Elisia was talking about.

Elisia looked to where the monster magpie had been perched a second ago, to find that it had departed.

Perhaps it was just her imagination.

"What was it, Elisia?"

"Nothing."

In her subconscious, alarm bells rang out as a phrase from a story, a poem perhaps, was recalled.

'One for sorrow.'

CHAPTER 11
BLACK CLOUDS

"Elisia, take the wheel, would you?"

"I—I've never taken the wheel before, of a ship,"

"It's easy," Thalt said simply.

"Dosvirians," Elisia muttered under her breath as they changed positions.

Thalt went over to check up on Borgian as Elisia grasped the wheel.

"He looks well, keep an eye on him for me."

"Why? where are you going?" Elisia asked Thalt.

"To find us some clothing, or for you, some drier clothing."

Elisia tutted, "Be quick then."

"Father, how did the departure go," Ariesa greeted her father, Mazdol.

"Well, Zensi's men are currently cleaning up the mess on the Rylus, many soldiers died and an archaeologist too, I believe."

"How? What happened?"

"Bandits, mercenaries, whatever you call them, they had taken over the ship, but it was reclaimed, the soldiers played their parts well."

"Sorry, their parts?" Ariesa wondered, suspicion began to gather.

"The soldiers' families will be paid handsomely, the agreed-upon amoun—"

"You did this, didn't you, why?"

"Well, for one, it distracted Zensi, so I can now act out the next phase of my plan, Elisia is gone so she cannot influence her husband to help Mezal, and Borgian and the barbarian, two people; one's allegiance bought by Zensi and the other, a friend, who could and would change my mind," Mazdol explained, "the mercenaries were soldiers dressed up like bandits from Borgian's previous camp, extra precaution, they played their parts amazingly, I even had pre-written lines by expert actors, produced for them in the case of them being threatened," he chuckled slightly.

"No, no, how could you?" Ariesa exclaimed with disbelief and hidden awe.

Stork, her brother, appeared behind her.

"What's wrong?"

"Nothing, just the act of liberation arriving in Mezal, nothing will stand in my way."

Mazdol clicked his fingers and the soldiers grabbed hold of Ariesa.

"What are you doing?" Stork shouted out as Ariesa was escorted to the prisons.

"It's the only place I know you'll stay in, and now, my son, prove to me your loyalty, the army is at your command, what say you?"

Stork shook his head at his father, ever so slightly, before he spoke the words.

"To war."

"You heard him, he is a Herginn, in blood is forged our eternal flame," Mazdol looked at his son.

The soldiers in the courtroom recognized him and repeated the clan's mantra.

"In blood is forged our eternal flame."

Thalt found clothing in the captain's cabin.

The clothing was elegantly embroiled with small slices of gem and woven from silks.

Thalt touched them and felt them before retrieving them in his hands.

As he took them, he glimpsed a soldier's armour among the chests of shoes on the cabinet's floor.

He rested the clothing he carried, down on the floor and removed the armour from its hiding place.

Emblazoned upon it were the signs of Clan Herginn, the boar and dagger.

Thalt returned it to the cabinet thinking nothing of it apart from the thought that he could, perhaps, wear it for protection upon the place of destination.

As it was returned, a small note fell from within the cuirass and onto the floor.

Thalt retrieved it and read it hastily:

To General Corvirin,

The plan can now go into action, the ship has been grounded and the previous sailors have been drowned in the river, the ship has been refurbished to look more like it was vehemently taken over, your bandit uniforms can be found on the top deck, it may be a good idea to put some soldiers into the positions of prisoners, and one last note to remember, should you meet your demise: in blood is forged our eternal flame,

Fight well,

Mazdol Herginn, Lord of Talgrin city, patriarchal Leader of Clan Herginn and rightful heir to the First Crown.

Thalt could not believe it, he rapidly rushed to the deck to tell Elisia of what he had just found out.

The pile of clothes lay on the floor still, forgotten for the moment.

When Elisia saw Thalt coming towards her so fast, she came away from the wheel and speedily went over to see what was wrong.

"What is it?" she asked.

"Mazdol, it was all planned from the start, read this."

Thalt handed her the note.

"Damn it, something was bound to happen soon but this, this is too soon, go find me some parchment and a quill, quickly."

Elisia was left waiting for only a couple minutes before he returned, with a roll of parchment paper, a rather battered-looking quill and a half-full inkwell.

She snatched them off him and began to write.

When she was done, she had Thalt read the finished letter.

It read as follows:

Dear Countess Zensi Alok,

It is with worry and misfortune, that I must inform you of Mazdol's plans, upon boarding the ship and setting off, we have found a note to one of Mazdol's generals describing the nature of his plan, the ship was taken over and then handed to Herginn soldiers disguised as bandits from Borgian's previous camp, it was a way of distracting everyone whilst getting rid of me so I could not persuade my husband to send you aid, I hope this letter reaches you in enough time, I fear he intends to attack Mezal.

Elisia Clairn, Countess of Drumdallg, Noble Wife of Bogstot Clairn of Clan Clairn

"It's enough," Thalt concluded after reading the letter.

"Enough? Let's hope 'enough' will do, any idea how we can get it to her?"

"I can only think of one, on all ships in Dosviri, on the lowest deck there used to always be a mechanism for emergency situations which letters could be sent through, they were known as Transmitters, they were illegalised though due to their incorporation of the arcane," Thalt exclaimed, "this ship may have one but it's doubtable."

Thalt took a heavy plank of firewood from the back of the ship and lodged it under the wheel of the ship to keep it on a steady course.

"This time, you can come."

"Welcome back, Countess Zensi."

Zensi didn't even need to see her to recognize who was addressing her: her friend and advisor, Georlia.

When Zensi did dismount, Georlia was guided by a soldier to Zensi.

Zensi thanked the soldier quietly and dismissed him before guiding Georlia herself.

"How are you?" Zensi asked.

"Well, your son proved himself as an able leader and heir in your absence," Georlia replied happily, "he needed little guidance from me."

"That is very good to hear," Zensi remarked.

There was a small silence in which the sound of illness could be heard.

"We noticed a problem whilst you were gone," Georlia looked somewhat worried.

"What is it?" Zensi spoke, sounding more worried than Georlia looked.

"We can't tell what it truly is, we've had alchemists, doctors, even historians and librarians come and inspect it."

"So, what is it?" Zensi inquired again.

"It's an epidemic, a rising plague, a scourge, it turns people. First, they die and then they come back, their skin as cold as ice and blue and green, deformed, the only knowledge of it that we know," Georlia paused, "is that it is connected to the Malice of Snow, no cure but to kill those who come back and have the healthy put away from the infected."

"Deformed..." Zensi focused on that one word and then she figured out why it resonated within her.

The prophecy.

"It's the next part of the prophecy," Zensi came out with, in realisation.

"How could I have not seen it before, what do we do, Zensi?"

"Stretch past the borders of Askaria, call every alchemist and doctor that will come," Zensi commanded.

"Of course, and how do I convince them to pass a border?" Georlia questioned Zensi.

Zensi stopped in her tracks, thinking, before finally coming to a decision, "How many Heads do we hold in the palace treasury?"

"Well, it still remains the largest in Askaria besides the Crowned Citadel's, it holds about 20,000 usable Heads."

"Only that many! I thought you said it was the largest treasury in Askaria, I'm in the middle of a war and I hold about as much money needed to buy four small merchant ships alone! Where has the rest of it gone?" Zensi exclaimed.

"Well, technically there are about 50,000 more Heads stored in there ... but they'll be gone in about a week," Georlia announced.

"Why?"

"It was the City Council's decision, a slave master from Targyrr offered 10,000 men trained in the art of war, for only 5 Heads each."

"So, we're now buying slaves from other kingdoms, are we? Slaves that our city cannot hold, slaves that our city cannot feed, did they even think to check with me!?"

"They didn't need to," Georlia told.

"Sorry, what do you mean?"

"They checked with your son as well as the Leader's Council, all agreed."

"Offer anyone who will come, the sum of 300 Heads, 500 if they know anything we don't about the Malice of Snow and this curse. I have a mess to sort out."

They walked down the stairs, a creak complimenting every board.

Thalt then remembered the prisoners, the ones that were soldiers, they had been forgotten for too long.

In the dim light of the torch Thalt held up, the broken bonds that had aided the soldier's prisoner disguises could be seen, scattered.

The soldiers had escaped, and they were still on the ship.

"Elisia, we have a problem."

"Hmm, well, can it wait, I think I've found the Transmitter," Elisia called back.

Thalt quickly rushed over and started inspecting the machine she had found.

"It looks in good condition, it's got half an arc cell left which should be plenty," Thalt opened a compartment at its front.

The machine was created from a dusty bronze and decorated with dark blue buttons, the compartment contained four circles of teal gem within it.

"The letter, if you please," Thalt requested the note addressed to Zensi.

Elisia passed him it and he placed it down on a pedestal in the compartment, the door was then shut on the piece of paper and an arrangement of buttons pressed—co-ordinates entered in.

The machine started to create a whirring sound and a cog on its side began to turn rhythmically, the machine continued like this for a minute or so before the door of the compartment was re-opened.

The note no longer lay on the pedestal.

"It worked?" Elisia wondered aloud.

"Yes, hopefully..."

Suddenly, from behind them, two silhouettes stepped forth and hit the pair unconscious with a metal bar.

"There's no going back now, we are sorry."

"No going back, you better hope those slaves are good and you better hope you can pay for their food," Zensi glared over at the Leader Council's representative, "don't ever do this again."

"It wasn't his fault, mother," Frienz exclaimed.

"No, it wasn't, it was whoever recognised the deal with this slaver," Zensi looked over at the City Council, "if you ever assume to manipulate members of the Leader's Council or the treasury of this city again, I will outcast every member of your organisation from my city, are we clear?"

"Yes, your greatness."

"Are the treasury keys still in your possessions; Mayk, Vlay, Aelius?"

"Yes," Vlay confirmed, presenting his key.

Vlay was commander of the guard within Mezal city.

"Then Aelius, if you could please deduct 50,000 Heads from the treasury and contain them in sacks. Vlay and Mayk, if you would accompany and help him."

Aelius God-Eyes was a humble and extremely well-informed man who looked very good for his age, he was late-fifties but looked more like he was in his early forties—he was one of the most trusted councillors in Mezal and a common acquaintance of Zensi's when it came to the subjects of economy and war and the legacy of Mezal.

"Of course," Aelius bowed and left the room.

In the old Ocularium of Mezal, a building dedicated, once, to receiving transmissions from ships and islands off land—a letter had been received.

"Queen Zensi! Queen Zensi!"

A courier suddenly burst through the door with something in his hand.

"What is it?"

"A message, a transmission," the courier replied.

"Elisia," Zensi exclaimed with instant realisation, "everyone, out."

Although a little stunned at first, everyone soon began to leave the room.

"A transmission, you say, clever."

The courier handed the letter over.

Zensi read it carefully, making sure not to leave out any detail.

"Mazdol. Mazdol," every time Zensi saw mention of the man's name on the letter, she would say it.

"What is it?" Georlia came in through the door, leaning on a long walking stick.

"Herginn planned the liberation of the ship, it was a distraction that should have lasted longer, however, is still worrying in its nature."

"What do we do, Zensi?"

"Set up a lookout down the Forgemaster's Path and set up more heavy guard patrols around Highstead, Stone Mount, Fort Callahere and Mezal."

Georlia nodded.

"We must be ready."

"So, what do we do with you two?" a rough-voiced man wondered.

"Well, did Lord Mazdol leave any information on what we're to do if we survive?" another man asked.

"What do you think? If he had, I would have already dealt with these two," the man snapped, looking at Elisia and Thalt who wore blindfolds over their eyes and rope around their wrists.

"You're a gem aren't ya, I wouldn't mind a few minutes of privacy alone with you in the captain's cabin," the rough-voiced man went over to Elisia and stroked her hair down to the lows of her back.

He licked his lips and had to be held back by the other man.

"We should be focusing on turning this ship around."

"And why would we do that, we're on course to a land of adventure and exploration, away from the wars of Askaria," the rough-voiced man illustrated his thoughts with his hands.

"Don't be an idiot, Bolgron Island is a land that no man would want to explore, all you need to know about it is in plain sight; it's a frozen wasteland of peril and disarray," the other tried to persuade the rough-voiced man who then proceeded to Thalt.

"How close are we to Bolgron, little man."

"About an hour before we arrive on the coast, enough time for me to have broken free from these binds and have wrapped my hands around both of your necks," Thalt smiled.

He was dealt a swift punch that freed blood from his nose and mouth.

It looked as if it did more damage to the man than him however, who tried to stifle his howls of pain.

"What in hell! What the fuck is your face made from? You fucking bastard!"

Elisia smirked, justified in doing so.

The rough-voiced man caught his breath.

"We only have an hour then, we'll continue on course and think of something to do with these ... these fuckers, on the way."

"I'll keep an eye on any changes in the weather, I don't like the look of that sky, black clouds are never a good omen."

Behind the wheel, Borgian awoke.

CHAPTER 12
BLOOD, STONE, SNOW

"Why such a quick dispatch, general? I was getting ready for dinner with my family when they told me I was required for lookout duty," the soldier asked as he sat down in front of the campfire.

The general was on the other side, cleaning his blade with a damp loincloth.

"Not completely sure myself, lad, something to do with a letter? But you can bet Herginn's involved," the general looked up at the soldier, "you can just be thankful that you were called when having dinner with your family, not anything else..."

The general pointed at a haggard man sitting against a tree, "You see that man over there."

"Yeah."

"You can be thankful you're were called whilst having dinner with your family because he was found in a brothel and certain event was interrupted for him to be here," the general chuckled, "I doubt the other lads will ever let him forget that."

"Let's hope they don't, an excuse to laugh in the future whilst we're fighting the war."

"We're fighting the war right now, lad, we're just not on the front lines."

The lookout was alive that night, with men struggling not to get too drunk on a crate of Dosvirian Red that one of the soldiers had snuck into the camp, and with the combined scents of boar and rabbit roasting on spits.

Spirits were high.

"I'd like to dedicate this one to Herginn, you great big fat plonker."

One of the soldiers, extremely drunk, had stood up with a lute and began strumming it ferociously and singing.

"We ... don't like you ... lord of Talgrin ... please ... fucking get killed ... and I won't ... I won't need to sing..."

He then started dancing dangerously close to the fire, everyone backed away.

"Roran, get away from there," one of the soldiers called out.

Drunk, Roran did not listen, he edged closer.

"Oh, Mazdol! Oh, Mazdol!" He continued to sing and edged ever forward.

"Roran, you drunken fool!"

The soldier who called out this time, slowly proceeded towards Roran.

"No! What're you doing!" the general called.

Roran then looked behind himself and saw the soldier approaching him.

Roran, in a drunken fury, then screamed, "Mazdol!" And grabbed a hot spit from the fire and drove it through the soldier's eye before losing his balance and falling into the flames of the campfire behind him.

The forest was filled with screams of anguish and men burned and bled.

Soldiers rushed to resolve the problem and continued to throw buckets of water over Roran, when he was eventually put out, his screams stopped.

He was still breathing and still alive until that steel-tipped length of wood plunged into the foreface of his head.

His breathing ceased and panic amassed.

More arrows followed.

More people died.

Figures, silhouettes began to creep from within the forest and surrounded the camp.

When they stepped into the light, their red armours could be clearly seen and the one man that lead them all, he was easy to identify.

He was Mazdol Herginn.

He drove a spear through the last man alive who played dead on the floor and then proceeded to pick up one of the bottles of Dosvirian Red that had fallen over.

He identified the label before popping the cap and taking a sip.

He immediately smashed the bottle on the floor.

"Dosvirians never could make wine," he commented, "onwards."

The soldiers trampled on over the corpses of foes they had never known the names of.

The sky was white, the waters foamed white as they climbed the coast, and the cliffs and the land before them, it was all white.

White, the colour of the snow that blanketed every inch of touchable land from the sands of the narrow beach to the tops of the large dead trees that touched the sky, atop their cliff resting places.

Borgian was the first to take sight of their destination, even whilst he laid down on the deck, could he see the tall, towering rock faces that stood like giants, watching over the lapping waves of the sea.

Borgian had been led in that position for approximately an hour now whilst awake; he had been waiting for an opportunity to attack.

The men who had taken Elisia and Thalt captive had not yet seen Borgian and Borgian hoped for it to remain that way until the moment of their deaths.

Only Thalt and Elisia joined him on deck at the current moment, the other men had disappeared down below.

"Psst ... psst ... over here."

"Borgian? You're awake?" Elisia's hushed voice sounded.

"We're at Bolgron?" Thalt questioned.

"Yes, to all of that ...who's at the wheel?" Borgian remembered a dilemma and looked at the wheel.

Borgian then stood up, he was risking it, but it was either this or death by drowning and having large splinters of wood driven through his body.

The plank of wood that Thalt had put under the wheel before had been dislodged and so Borgian took hold of the wheel.

It was surprisingly smooth under his hands and with it, he steered the ship away from its direct course of destruction towards the cliffs.

The ship gently rocked on the coast and eventually came to a stop.

"Okay, let's get off this ship," Borgian called out.

He rushed down the length of the ship, limping from the arrow wound in his leg, and revealed his trusty blade—he cut his companions loose and undid their blindfolds.

"Thanks," Thalt exclaimed as he moved towards the side of the ship and began dismounting, using wooden steps embedded in the hull.

Borgian and Elisia followed and as soon as all dismounted, the chilling cold was felt.

The sand was white with the layer of snow blanketing it.

"Where do we head?" Borgian asked.

Thalt replied, "North and west, the city of Val'Vhere isn't far in that direction."

"Val'Vhere?" Elisia questioned.

"The city where Rolgirtis the Blue Knight would have ruled from."

"Well, let's get a move on," Borgian suggested.

"And the ship?" Elisia looked back at the wooden structure.

"We'll have to hope they're gone for when we get back otherwise, we kill them, simple."

Night had fallen over Askaria, it provided the perfect cover for Mazdol and his small army along the way to Mezal.

Their banners hung high and a battle formation had been assembled, it would be an infiltration until the gates of the inner Forering needed to be passed, then it would become a storming.

The gates of Mezal had already been opened by a man inside the Forering, who was promised he could keep his life during the attack if he left straight away.

Mazdol's army swept the place, killing the unwary and burying their weapons in the enemy.

The army proceeded to the inner gates and smashed through them, equipping their combined weight against the doors.

It was after this that the emergency bells rang out.

The soldiers flooded in through the streets.

Mazdol leading them all and killing anyone standing in their way.

Every cobble was painted red.

No person left untouched by the cold steel of a blade.

The city was within their grasp, and all that was left to take now was the palace...

"Mazdol! I can't let you through here," Commander Vlay shouted out at the palace gates, accompanied by a horde of soldiers.

"Vlay, you insignificant peasant, eventually you'll learn," Mazdol retorted.

"You may be far from a pauper, Mazdol, but your wealth does not make up for the fact you are explicitly dumb and lacking in any achievement, except for starting a war, if you call that an achievement."

"I have started a war that I will win, and it will be a day of celebration and mocking and bountiful execution; a pity that you won't be alive to see it," Mazdol looked at Vlay with happy, evil eyes before unsheathing his silver axe, Myrmidon.

"Into the fray, men," Vlay shouted before him and his soldiers ran into battle.

Vlay instinctively went for Mazdol, a decision that would seal his fate, and was dealt with swiftly.

Vlay attempted the first blow unsuccessfully and had it deflected, he was knocked back, and then Mazdol swung his axe.

Vlay jumped back in just enough time to only receive a small tear in his mail.

Mazdol continued forwards and progressed to swing a more successful blow, this time he drew blood from Vlay's torso.

Vlay hissed in pain.

A few seconds later, Mazdol's axe was in Vlay's skull.

Vlay was sound.

The way was clear.

Mazdol smiled.

Val'Vhere was a city of vast size.

Almost as soon as the trio had made their way to the snowy surface atop the cliffs, it had become visible.

The venture there was to, thankfully, be a short one however still met with danger.

About halfway there, did they encounter their first taste of how the Malice of Snow had affected the island...

"Rather barren, isn't it," Borgian remarked, staring across the white, snowy plains whilst keeping his attention on the satisfying crunching sound the snow made as they walked across it.

"Well, you'd expect it to be after all that's happened here; a paralysing cold, a debilitating plague, ruthless armies and angry gods, it's a miracle that Val'Vhere hasn't completely fallen to ruin," Elisia replied.

Borgian didn't respond, he continued to listen to the crunching sound they all made as they traversed the snowy land.

After a while, as they began to near the city, did the crunching sound stop, they still walked on snow but the sound seemed to be muffled.

It sounded wrong.

Borgian looked down upon noticing this and froze in his tracks.

"Borgian? What is it?" Thalt asked.

When Borgian didn't answer, Thalt and Elisia also began to look downwards.

They saw what he saw.

And what he was seeing were the frozen faces of the dead, their skin: a green, unhealthy tone, beyond their other skin of the icy surface above.

The ground was completely formed of a layer of frozen corpses.

"Gods above..." Elisia exclaimed.

"And here lie the great White Elves of Bolgron Island."

Val'Vhere had no gates, the city probably had a pair of them at some point but not now, they had most likely been ripped off by the violent, snow-plagued winds carried by the curse.

The trio wandered cautiously in, with the eerie feeling that someone or something was watching them.

The streets were filled with snow, houses buried beneath it.

It seemed that an icy layer had formed over the snow allowing the trio to stay atop ground.

The Pearl Palace was a short distance away from where they were.

It was where they were headed, imagining that it would hold some sort of record of information.

Noises echoed from within the city.

Eerie and unnatural.

"I imagine this place would have been beautiful," Thalt thought aloud, "at some point, maybe when it wasn't destroyed and flooded with snow and ice."

"Hard to imagine it without the snow, I mean these buildings are made of gold and marble," Elisia exclaimed.

"They sure don't look it," Borgian remarked, looking up at the greyish, snow-blanketed buildings.

The city was like something from a nightmare that hadn't been realised as one yet.

"The snow's weird enough itself, isn't it?" Borgian stared into the snow, noticing how slow it fell.

"It's scarce in Askaria as it is only in the Cold. It's weird seeing this amount."

A noise sounded overhead for a few seconds, like a roar, but distant and undeveloped.

"What was that?" Elisia stopped to acknowledge the sound.

"A bear?" Borgian suggested.

"Surely, it wouldn't survive in this climate," Elisia countered.

"No, Elisia's right, that definitely wasn't a bear," Thalt confirmed.

"Then, what was it?" Borgian awaited an answer from Thalt.

"Something much bigger."

Something stirred a building nearby, causing something to smash.

"Time to move?" Borgian proposed.

Thalt nodded, keeping his eyes fixed on the building where the smashing sound had emitted from.

Elisia had already started moving in the direction of the palace once again.

The wind had picked up, a stench of death circulated around Mezal city, the streets salivated with blood, the moon glared upon the place.

The red demons had crept in.

The doors of Zensi's palace were ripped from their hinges and threw to the floor, the staunch Herginn soldiers ran over the bodies of the unsuccessful Alok supporters.

Mazdol breathed in the cold night's air and smelt the fires burn and the blessed miasma of adrenaline and flesh.

He was already successful, he could feel it in his bones, in his veins, he would purge this city, and the rest of Askaria next.

And so, would his bloodline...

"Father, Fort Callahere has been secured, we are victorious," Stork Herginn and his soldiers amassed before Mazdol.

Mazdol embraced his son.

"Victory," Mazdol whispered at first, "victory!" he then shouted to rouse his men.

His soldiers cheered all around him.

"Now, get your filthy arses in there and rip me out somebody's heart."

Mazdol's soldiers ran in, excited to fulfil his request.

Mazdol strutted down the narrow halls of the longhouse like he already owned the place, following his soldiers.

His son followed him.

All the soldiers proceeded through a secret doorway into the courtroom but Mazdol decided he'd rather take the main entrance with a small group of guards.

At the end of the hall, lit dimly by candles and dusty in places, the door to Zensi's courtroom stood closed and guarded by a soldier.

"May I enter," Mazdol asked softly upon approaching with more than a hint of smugness in his voice.

"Sorry, Lord Herginn, orders are to not let you and your associates in here unless a council meeting is taking place, I am bound by my orders," the soldier announced nervously.

The way he spoke, told Mazdol that he quite obviously was unaware of the situation taking place outside.

As well as this, Mazdol also took note of the soldier's nervousness.

Mazdol knew exactly how to deal with the nervous: intimidation.

"Do you know what else is bound, my dagger in its sheath but that can change oh so easily, have you ever felt the cold of steel on your forehead."

The soldier quivered.

Mazdol was about to draw his knife before the soldier drew his sword.

"What a shame, and I was going to take it easy on you," Mazdol tutted before now, reaching for his favourite, brutal, axe: Myrmidon.

At this, the soldier, in a strange turn of events, opened the doors and dropped his sword and pleaded with his eyes and his trembling bottom lip, not to be killed.

Mazdol knew no sort of mercy and slammed the soldier's head into the wall, a trickle of blood ran down the soldier's face.

"Was that necessary?" Stork shouted.

"What do you mean! How many people did you kill whilst at the fort, hmm, you're still soft!" Mazdol shouted, slightly taken aback by his son's hesitance to watch Mazdol kill the enemy, "you need to learn that not everyone survives, in fact, this soldier, he's still alive but—"

Mazdol slammed his axe into the unconscious soldier's head, a fountain of blood gushed from the wound as the axe was removed.

"Now, he's dead, he didn't survive."

Stork proceeded hesitantly onwards as his father stayed behind.

Mazdol spat on the soldier's face and walked over the corpse, into the courtroom.

Zensi Alok awaited Mazdol, with her soldiers, her steward, Georlia, and her son, Frienz.

Zensi Alok spoke, "Mazdol Herginn, is power such a drink that you cannot quench your thirst on any other luxury."

Mazdol then shouted, "I am afraid so, my dear! Power has become a drink I am rather fond of and one that I savour, taking one sip at a time until I reach the bottom of my glass which I assure you, will take me and my descendants a very long time, thankfully time and the money to buy the drink, are two things I have," Mazdol looked around the room, "I don't know about you lot and you, Zensi but I think I'll finish up with my glass when a certain crown lies on my head and a certain woman lies bleeding on the ground with a silver spear through her back, the same way my father died. I will not rest until all of your bloodline has soaked into the ground and the Council Moot knows their true leader, your city is taken, you are nothing."

Zensi laughed and her soldiers laughed with her.

"Come now Mazdol, the city will be retaken, you are outnumbered, more than fifty soldiers stand here," Zensi's son, Frienz, spoke.

"Really? Because I count one hundred and two, precisely."

Suddenly, out of the shadows, Mazdol's soldiers appeared with spears, bows, blades, cleavers and axes.

Zensi and her soldiers were already beat, she knew this but either way, she'd still strive to lay at least one cut into Mazdol's flesh: "Kill them, leave no man you can fight, un-fought!"

The battle began, and blood ran the length of the court's floor in only a few seconds, Zensi and Mazdol both weaved their way through the mayhem to each other and when they did, they conversed again.

"You know your end draws near," Mazdol took a step forward.

"Can you clarify just how near my end is for me?" Zensi gave a small, mocking smile, "you've been saying my end's been near for ages and yet it's never been delivered so tell me now, how near?."

She took a step forward.

"Soon, but not today, as soon as I have stripped you of everything you have, starting with your city and then your people and then your son. Then will you finally die," Mazdol held his position.

"Ah ... an empty promise, I'm sure, you know that no clan will join your side for fear of what you'll do if they fail."

"And no clan will admit to joining your side for fear of what I'll do to them."

Zensi shook her head slowly, still smiling, "But they've admitted to me, can you say the same? Where will your allies be when you lie in the ground?"

Zensi discreetly revealed a sharpened knife from its scabbard, she could sense this conversation was coming to a close.

Mazdol gave a short chuckle before announcing, "Worry about yourself. What comes next, you won't survive."

Mazdol reached for Myrmidon but Zensi was already a step ahead of him, she dug her knife deep into his arm where the wound sent blood spraying like a sprinkler.

Mazdol screamed in agony and as he did, it seemed Zensi's remaining soldiers fell dead immediately.

Mazdol's soldiers rushed to support him, they restrained Zensi's arms.

She didn't fight them, she knew this would happen and she was just happy for now ... watching Mazdol struggle with his deep, ugly wound.

"Take them to the prison in Talgrin and return my family safely back to the longhouse and once more, I will say, do not let Ariesa out! Find my healer and kill Zensi's soldiers and only kill the citizens if they do not submit to my leadership, I control the council, the kingdom and the crown."

Mazdol stared at Zensi as she was dragged away, he smiled, showing her his glee.

"Enjoy this time, Mazdol, I will reclaim my city."

Mazdol thought to himself as he watched his soldier's swords release spurts of blood from the heads of Zensi's injured soldiers, "I highly doubt it."

"How far now?" Borgian inquired.

"On the other end of this street," Elisia replied, "you can see it over the roofs."

"The tower?" Borgian wondered.

Thalt nodded, "It's made by elves, it's bound to look strange."

"They like to make everything look like towers, don't they?" Borgian realised.

Elisia laughed a little, "They do like their towers."

The palace was a thing of beauty, it was perhaps the only beautiful thing in the city.

It was a spiralling structure with hundreds of balconies and gold shields and blue sapphires embedded into its marble walls.

The gate was even more so extravagant, carved from opaque quartz, and with hinges of pure silver, with pearls and tourmaline, morion and a single large amethyst decorating the door.

It looked extremely heavy and it was.

The combined strengths of the trio could not make it budge and it was only when Elisia's hand slipped and pushed down on the amethyst, did the doors open.

The sound the doors of the huge gate made was horrible, a terrible grating sound that caused the three to briefly bring their hands to their ears to stifle the sound.

"Well, that wasn't great," Borgian commented before walking forward into the Pearl Palace.

The sight before them was a strange one, even before they had reached the centre of the building, could they see the gaping hole they were approaching and the pedestal on which a book sat, before the pit.

The trio advanced with caution.

Borgian went to pick up the book but hesitated, he waited for a second or two before finally collecting the book.

There were no traps as Borgian previously thought there might have been.

He flipped through the book but there was nothing.

He then passed it to Thalt who asked for it, he found something.

"One page, four words," he said plainly, he showed the page to Borgian and Elisia.

It read: Amateir-Tourjest-Gothrog-Ethril

"Amateir, Clan Amateir of the Sundered Isles?" Borgian recalled some knowledge.

"What do the other words mean?" Elisia pondered aloud.

There came no reply.

Elisia then took the book from Thalt and spotted something the others didn't, on the next page.

It read simply: Don't disturb the revenant of the pit, on reckoning day will it arise. Use this book, it is your saviour, return it to your land. Let those worthy, read.

She showed the others, and they all edged towards the large, gaping hole.

They stared over the edge and saw the Revenant.

In a frozen capsule, did the skyscraper-sized, giant, Revenant stand frozen, with twisted horns and sharp nails and a face that was but a skull.

Borgian noticed the capsule seemed to be melting.

"Well, apparently we have a saviour, this book, should we return?"

"Yes, I've had enough of this apocalyptic city," Borgian confirmed, "there's a chill in my bones that I don't want sticking there."

CHAPTER 13
FROM THE HEARTLAND

The trio left the city with haste, they knew they'd find no other help there, the sun was setting, and a northerly wind was picking up.

The snow had become heavier...

Val'Vhere looked even more so apocalyptic at night and so, they were inclined to walk faster.

When they had left the gates of the city, was when they noticed something strange: the whole layer of snow before them had been trampled, footsteps and imprints left in the snow like a stampede of people had hurried over it.

A groaning sound emitted in the distance, it was followed by a clicking noise and a rushing sound.

Borgian suddenly drew his blade, "Something's not right."

Everyone else drew their weapons as they took sight of movement not far away.

"Could it be the men from the ship?" Thalt wondered.

No one answered, the three moved forward.

Slowly.

On the road that had now come visible under the trampled snow.

And then, did they take sight of something, and it was a something, that much was sure but what it was, exactly, was unknown.

It was a hulking beast, the ridges of its spine sticking out from its pale blue, leathery, skin-tight back.

Its ears were enlarged and pointed and even in the crouched position it now retained, it could be seen that it was too large, too abnormal, to be human—or elv…

Nobody dared say a word, in case the beast heard them.

The trio exchanged worried looks before Thalt proceeded to instinctively creep up on the beast, he revealed his twin daggers and raised them above the beast before plunging them downwards.

The creature suddenly ceased what it was doing, and it could be seen, that it had been feasting.

It turned around to confront Thalt.

Its face was one out of a nightmare, its eyes were like slits with dark blue eyes hidden within, its mouth was pulled across its face which was shaped like an elongated, upside-down egg.

The colour of its face was a pale blue and instead of hands, it bore spears of flesh.

Borgian recognised what it was.

"The Disavowed."

Borgian shouted out, "Run!"

He knew there was no way to kill the pure Disavowed of legend.

Borgian and Elisia began to run straight away, Borgian looked back once to see the Disavowed clamp its jaws together and bring its knife-like teeth to a close over Thalt's neck.

His whole head was removed and in one swallow-gone.

"Shit!" Borgian exclaimed.

"What just happened?"

"I … I don't know," Borgian heaved for breath whilst talking, "Thalt's dead."

"Gods above."

When they decided that they were safe, Borgian and Elisia stopped at the cliff's edge, the waves lapped below, sparkling with the setting sun.

"The ship's still there," Elisia noted.

"The men won't be there though, I have a feeling they were what the creature was eating," Borgian realised.

Elisia pulled a face and then progressed towards the beach, Borgian followed.

They started to walk faster once the growling sounds returned, echoing from the distance.

They began to run once again when not one, but a whole horde of the Disavowed appeared on the horizon.

"To the ship!"

They ran down the decline from cliff to beach, the Disavowed not far behind them now.

The beasts were much quicker than they were.

When they reached the ship, they quickly ascended the ladder on the hull.

The Disavowed could be seen edging ever forwards, now also on the beach.

Elisia and Borgian mounted the ship and drew up the anchor.

The wheel was equipped, and the ship slowly cast off but not in enough time to escape from the creatures.

They scraped the wood and smashed holes in the hull, thankfully, not low down enough to take in water.

As Borgian drove the ship, Elisia tried to stop the Disavowed from climbing the side of the ship by throwing heavy planks of wood over the side.

Eventually, they succeeded in escaping from the coast, the Disavowed stopped following, and like zombies, retreated up the coast, towards something.

In the darkness of the night that crept upon Bolgron, Borgian was sure he caught sight of a dark knight, Rolgirtis.

The symbol on Borgian's hand began to glow and a pain ran through it, one he hadn't felt since Sesan.

The ship had departed and set sail home, back to Askaria.

CHAPTER 14
NOT THE SAME

A group of soldiers had awaited Borgian and Elisia's return.

What surprised Borgian, was that they were all dressed in red.

And they were not the only things dressed in red, on the journey to Mezal, through Slaa Valley, Borgian noticed that the few houses there, bore red banners along with the Alok Estate Tower.

Something had happened whilst he was gone.

Something big.

When Borgian and Elisia first took sight of Mezal city, they both noticed the differences, there were gaps in the walls, houses with smoke rising from them and the main gate had been decorated with hanging soldier's heads and the walls, red with the banners of Clan Herginn.

Borgian was sure he knew what had happened, it was obvious what had happened, from the soldiers in dark scarlet that greeted them upon arrival and the bloodied ground.

The roses were red, the dead were red, the blood was red.

Mazdol had taken over Mezal city.

Mazdol sat atop the Throne of Mezal in front of the council table that had newly been relocated to the Palace Hall.

When he saw them, he stood up to welcome and to talk, "Borgian, Elisia, you have returned, welcome to Herginn-influenced Mezal city, I am sure you've already gathered what has happened and…"

Mazdol seemed lost in his own thoughts for a moment, "news, what news do you bring, how was the endeavour?" Mazdol questioned, suddenly remembering himself.

Borgian passed the book to Mazdol.

"We found this."

"Hmmm..." Mazdol was thinking, "it doesn't make any sense to me, however there is a man, Aelius God-Eyes, he lives at the end of the city. He used to be very close to the Alok family, but I have convinced him of his mistakes or at least I hope so, he is a fountain of information and so, useful."

Mazdol passed the mysterious book back to Borgian.

"I'll take it to Aelius, my lord," Borgian told as he saw the glint of power in Mazdol's eyes.

"Borgian, my friend, we are men of the same land, we must treat each other as equals, I am no lord to you as long we remain truthful to one another."

Elisia gave Mazdol a look, "We know that's a lie, you're the type to have someone's head mounted on a spike if they forgot to address you as lord."

Mazdol returned a glare, "I saw the letter you sent, Elisia, you were clever to find out about my plan but dumb to sign the letter. Today, you live, tomorrow, you die."

"Mazdol, don't start more wars, the gods know they are not needed," Borgian spoke to Mazdol.

Elisia gave Borgian a slight nod of appreciation, remembering that he probably knew nothing of the letter and yet, said nothing about it, it made Elisia look less alone in her struggle here.

"I don't intend to start wars, Borgian, I intend to finish them, what I have done recently is a great step in ending this war," Mazdol snapped.

"And provoking the next," Elisia brought forth.

"I have done more than that whore ever did whilst she ruled this city! I have had twenty-three doctors visit here from all over, to try their hand at curing this plague in the city, people are dropping like flies!" Mazdol barked.

"And what would encourage such a kindness? Surely, they weren't here for just the people," Elisia queried.

At that, Mazdol suddenly, involuntarily, clenched his arm.

"Gods above, you really have got the plague," She half chuckled, "perhaps, there's a chance for Askaria, after all."

Mazdol scowled at her and stood up, disgraced, "You have a death wish, woman and I'll be happy to fulfil it, when everything is over with, when I'm cured, you and your oaf of a husband can expect war."

"We'll be ready," she reassured him before turning to Borgian, "good luck, Borgian, I hope we shall meet again soon."

As she turned to leave, she suddenly stopped and gave Mazdol the middle finger, "As for you I hope you die and drown in your own blood and vomit, bastard."

Then, she left.

"It was Zensi who gave me this plague," Mazdol exclaimed.

"How?" Borgian asked him.

"She cut me," he explained in a sentence.

Mazdol dismounted his throne properly and edged towards Borgian, revealing his revolting wound under a linen bandage.

It wasn't small, and it was full of puss and blood, dried and fresh.

The excessive amount of dried puss within was helping to keep the wound more widely open.

It smelt putrid and made Borgian feel like retching.

Before Borgian had to ask for Mazdol to put the bandage back over the wound, he had rewrapped it in its linen.

"The city lent me this plague and I hope now, that if we get rid of this curse, so will the plague disappear with it," Mazdol stated.

"Don't count on it. At Bolgron, we had an encounter with some of those who had been diseased, Thalt didn't survive."

"If they can kill the ex-commander of the emperor's own elite guard, I'm worried about what they will do to simple soldiers," Mazdol took a breather, "well, you best get some sleep, you must be tired."

"Yes, I'm bloody exhausted, I will," Borgian confirmed, "oh, and one last thing, just be careful, please don't get yourself killed over something as immaterial as a crown."

Mazdol grimaced at Borgian, "I can't make any promises."

Outside, the night was crisp, stars like small ghostly lanterns, the moon like an angel's face and the overwhelming darkness like a giant's shadow.

Borgian inhaled the cold air and he thought, would he be able to stop the upcoming danger? Or would, for eternity, this land of greed and blood be sentenced to infinite frost and woeful winter?

He remembered the frozen beast he had seen in the pit at Bolgron Island, he couldn't fight that or at least not without the superpower he'd gain from whatever the clues in the book, would lead him to.

He had not expected what had happened to Sesan and if he had known what the sword could do ... and then he thought, he knew exactly what the sword could do and that was why he wanted it.

Even he had become prey to the dangerous aura of want, around Askaria.

But he knew, he could still redeem himself, there was still time to cease the fury of the snow.

CHAPTER 15
SHORT SENTENCED

Frienz Alok, the heir to Mezal city's throne after his mother, or would have been heir if not for Mazdol, felt the prison walls for any sign of secret passageway.

He could feel the presence of his anxious mother, Zensi, through the wall.

He was desperate to escape.

Clan Herginn had taken over Mezal city too easily, there had to be a flaw in the plan.

Frienz looked down at his aching hands, they were covered in a mixture of dry and fresh blood along with cuts and broken skin from trying to find an exit, the rough wall had scraped his hands of many layers of skin.

As soon as Frienz decided to give up and take a rest, a brick came loose.

Frienz walked over and put his hand in the hole, he felt around, there was nothing and then suddenly the whole wall fell, a brick narrowly avoided Frienz's foot.

As the dust cleared, a large group of sweating serval soldiers bearing the greens of Clan Alok could be seen along with many of the surviving soldiers of Mezal, from a secret tunnel.

"We must get my mother and her steward," Frienz ordered as the loyalists rushed in, they attached hooks to the door and attached ropes to them, and pulled.

The doors came down and Frienz stepped out to see the loyalists do the same with the doors of the other cells.

As Zensi and Georlia came out from their cells, so did Herginn guards from their posts down the corridor.

One of the loyalists pointed to the tunnel behind the ruins of the wall, "Go, we'll hold them off!"

Frienz, Georlia and Zensi rushed down the passageway, not needing to be told twice.

Soon enough, torchlight came slipping around the corner along with the sound of swords clinking and the eventual noise of the spurt of the blood from the wounds of both Herginn and Alok soldiers alike.

Zensi beckoned the old blind woman, Georlia, to keep up but she quickly tired and slipped, her ragged prisoner robes became stained with the dirt of the ground she fell onto.

The Herginn soldiers caught up with her easily, they grabbed her arms as she thrashed, trying to escape their grip, but it was unavoidable, they restrained her, and she was hauled away.

The soldiers seemed to forget about Zensi and Frienz who managed to escape, their hands grappled onto the grassy parchment of land that now lay above them and they were free.

Talgrin city mocked them still though, Clan Herginn had Georlia.

"Damn every evil Dycrite god," Zensi shouted.

"Damn Herginn and damn the power lust, damn the stupid crown."

Frienz did not know what to say as he could not tell any words of comfort for he knew nothing to happen to Georlia, would be good and comforting.

"Send a message to our man in Mezal, gather all the loyalists around Askaria and rally, war is coming."

CHAPTER 16
GOD-EYES

A smell of old incense lifted Borgian's senses.

Borgian had entered Aelius's shack, it was built crudely from wood and looked very out of place among the stone houses of the city, it was carpeted with hay and lit by small lamps, casting shadows around the room.

Borgian proceeded in and entered a room decorated with threads of garlic, large colourful feathers and pieces from a broken mirror, dangling from the roof.

Aelius God-Eyes was sat in the corner on a creaking chair, next to him was a young woman standing patiently, this woman was brown-haired and brown-eyed, she was Aelius's daughter.

"Borgian Steel, ah, we've been expecting you, Mazdol's soldiers tell me you have a book, please, give it to me."

Borgian passed the book to the slightly age-wrinkled, blue-eyed man.

Aelius put his ear to the book before opening it carefully.

"I can hear how old the book is, it was written in the first age whilst a great danger took place, the words, they can only be deciphered to one end, they are words of the elves," Aelius looked at the book once more as if to double-check before continuing, "it means, from what I know about the elves, that Gothrog the Coal King, brother of King Rolgirtis, lies in the Great Cavern of Tourjest protecting the Ethril Blade, the only sword powerful enough to challenge the Malice of Snow and it's controller. To open Tourjest Cavern would require a descendant of Clan Amateir of the City of Amateir of the Sundered Isles, I happen to know who you seek."

"Father, these are secrets held sacred by our family, only us and Clan Amateir alone are meant to know about Tourjest," the woman next to Aelius reminded.

"Ah, yes, of course my dear daughter but Arntia, Clan Amateir are known for their wisdom, surely with the curse that ravages this land, they will know that they must sacrifice certain things to get rid of a danger that, even if the whole of life on Askaria was sacrificed, would still destroy what's left," Aelius reasoned.

"I suppose that makes sense," Arntia nodded.

Borgian pulled a slightly confused face.

"You show promise, Borgian Steel, but what should I expect in return for my services, every man has his terms, I hope you have not forgotten," Aelius peered at Borgian, awaiting an answer.

"I'd be in your debt, anything you need," Borgian gave his word.

Aelius smiled, "That will suffice, I will arrange a meeting with you and the heir of Clan Amateir, he's a dear friend of mine, expect him in the Nestled Crow Inn tomorrow night."

"Thank you," Borgian gave his gratitude.

Aelius nodded, "Keep aware always Borgian, the mortal devil of the Dycrite lie inside the city, and outside, on your journey, more, and a man who has little soul must stay vigilant."

CHAPTER 17
UNSEEN

Borgian was readying himself in the private armoury along with Lord Bogstot Clairn and a few soldiers chosen to accompany the group on the task ahead.

Bogstot had volunteered to come along.

For the time being, it seemed Mazdol could stomach Bogstot enough to allow him in the city.

No one was completely sure what Gothrog the Coal King was and the danger he posed, which was why the guards were provided.

Before all, however, Aron Amateir needed to be sought out, Borgian could remember riding past the Nestled Crow Inn before in one of his travels, it lied at the edge of the eastern part of the Forelands; there was only one route and it was dangerous.

Borgian stepped out of his thoughts, the sound of a blade sliding out of its sheath, startled him.

"Come Steel, we must practise if we wan' to stand a chance against the beasts that lie ahead," Bogstot offered.

"Let's," Borgian accepted.

Borgian released his sword from its protector.

Borgian and Bogstot continued to clash their blades until Bogstot span his sword quickly but with all his strength and bashed his weapon against Borgian's, Borgian's sword flew from his hands.

Bogstot put his hand to Borgian, Borgian grasped it and was pulled back to his feet.

"Got to improve yer footin'," Bogstot informed Borgian.

Noticing the setting sun, the group decided to set off to the inn.

Night fell quickly and Borgian began to worry, moonlight struck the brows of the trees, stars littered the black night, the road had disappeared into the forest's shadows and no light or sign of life could be seen.

The forest that they had entered was recognised by Borgian as Arihsa Der, a land once owned by Goblins and Dwarves an age ago.

In history, at the Battle of Der, Goblins and Dwarves fought for dominion over the beautifully superior Underwood as it was known then.

During the battle, they realized the destruction they were inflicting on the area so they both decided to share the land in harmony and to rebuild, the forest was renamed Arihsa Der, translating to Land of Acceptance.

Borgian was hoping for the appearance of the inn soon, but as the trees seemed to cluster closer, they began to lose hope.

"Should we stop."

One of the guards made Borgian jump.

"No, not here, too dangerous."

Borgian noticed his breath, so cold he could see it now, like a wisp of white smoke, he was also out of breath, tired too.

"Are you ok, sir?" One of the soldiers inquired.

"I'm good," Borgian turned to Bogstot, "where are we exactly?"

"Don't know, didn' bring a map," Bogstot announced.

"Shit," Borgian exclaimed, "I hate these forests."

An owl hooted somewhere amongst the trees.

"What was that?" Borgian could hear something besides owls, getting louder and louder.

"Just an owl," Bogstot put blandly.

"No."

Borgian listened closer.

He could hear them now, hooves.

"It's a horse," Borgian exclaimed.

"He's right," a soldier confirmed, "look, the steed's as black as night, wait ... the rider ... oh, gods above."

"Get down!" Bogstot shouted suddenly.

Borgian heeded the warning, ducking down and rolling slightly, into a bush.

Borgian saw one guard still on the path, caught unawares.

Borgian could see the all-feared rider now.

It was a creature of horror, its face could be seen, featureless and formed of bloody muscle and sinew, it was tall as well, taller than many creatures Borgian had seen and had eyes of violet, its legs had been replaced by a conjoining of tendons attached to the horse.

The horse was made of flesh-stripped bones and rotting entrails with hooves of rusted iron, it bore no head, just a stump.

What was this thing?

It was like an undead centaur but with the whole horse's body besides the head.

Suddenly, the creature let out a clicking sound from two holes, one on either side of its face, they looked strangely like mouths.

From out of its scabbard, came a great rusting blade which it plunged into the unwary guard's chest, blood painted the trees red as it spurted, and the corpse of the guard fell back into the dirt that soaked up the scarlet liquid.

Borgian muttered, "Rest in peace," under his breath, he was whinnying a little after the horrifying display, but it only got worse...

The figure dismounted its horse and elevated the corpse up, Borgian thought he saw life return to the soldier's body for a mere moment and then, to confirm this, the soldier turned towards the bush where Borgian hid, with a pained and helpless expression etched on his face.

Somehow the creature had resurrected the guard but only briefly.

The creature placed one hand on the guard's head and gripped before swiftly tearing the whole head of the soldier, clean off.

Bogstot retched and the gory, blood-covered, creature turned quickly around to face Borgian's hiding place, it extended a long, thin arm that kept on going.

Borgian considered its face; its two violet, motionless pupils.

Borgian drew his sword and readied it, he saw what looked like Bogstot's bulky silhouette, edging back in the neighbouring piece of shrubbery.

A twig snapped where Bogstot hid and the creature lost interest in Borgian, it would have discovered Bogstot if not for a white arrow shot from above, piercing the creature where its heart would be, if it had one.

The creature exploded in golden flames.

Borgian tried to see the group's saviour but his vision was too blurred and a searing pain across his arm distracted him, he looked down, an arrow dripping with blue liquid—poison, was stuck in his arm.

Borgian attempted pulling it out but it was too far in, dark and light flashed before him and he saw a vision of snow, his time was running out...

Borgian's efforts were worth nothing to the Blue Knight

CHAPTER 18
THE GOOD POISON

"Wake up! Wake up! Wake up!"

Borgian quickly sat up and slowly took in the scene, he was on an uncomfortable, dirtied bed, lying down in a room.

The wallpaper was peeling off the walls and a musky scent stunk out the location, he was in an inn, perhaps—the inn.

Elisia Clairn was standing over him, "Thank the prayers, I thought I overdid the amount of poison for a moment, I feared you would lie asleep forever."

Borgian then remembered the previous happenings, the arrow in the arm, the creature, Borgian had many questions but he was going to ask this first.

"What was the creature, that thing?"

Elisia opened her mouth to speak but the familiar voice of Bogstot sitting up in a bed opposite Borgian, came first.

"Tha' was a wraith, dark spirits that used to be people, users of dark magic, now, they are Draugr who wander and take heads to devour the knowledge of life or so they believe, it was lucky me clever wife followed us."

"Why did you poison us?" Borgian turned to Elisia.

"I expected at least one of you to have seen the creature's eyes, I had to put you to sleep so your veins would stop pumping the darkness into your blood, I had to extract it, cut it out before it killed you."

Borgian looked at his bandaged wrist and then to the bedside table, a jar of black sticky substance lay inside, Borgian expected that to be the darkness.

"It had almost killed you, a clever trick from the wraiths," Elisia paused for a moment before concluding, "you seem alright now though and if you do truly feel well enough, an Aron Amateir would like to meet you downstairs, oh, and you better get dressed first."

Borgian suddenly noticed his nudity and that his clothing and armour were piled on the floor, he put them on quickly, under his covers, unlike Bogstot who had no fear and did it all to the extremity that Borgian had to turn around.

On leaving the room, Borgian said to Elisia, "Looks like I have yet another debt to repay."

Elisia waved him down, "No, it's on the house, so to speak."

Borgian kissed her hand as manors decreed.

"Keep safe, won't you, Askaria's a dangerous place, especially with your reputation, ex-bandit," Elisia gave a caring look, "it was good seeing you again."

"Don't worry about me, you've got your husband to take care of," Borgian smiled.

"Oy! I can take care of myself," Bogstot commented from the back of the room,"

Elisia blushed during a drawing-on silence between Borgian and her.

"Well, I will be off, thank you," Borgian finished.

"Wait, keep wary of Herginn for me, will you, don't trust him for a second."

Borgian nodded and closed the door behind him, and Bogstot who followed.

He headed downstairs, Bogstot clunking, not far behind.

On the bottom floor, were many happy people, a large portion of them drunk to the point they would be sick now and again, making the cleaners very unhappy.

Business seemed to be booming.

"I'm goin' to get a drink, or two," Bogstot announced as he lost himself in the crowd.

"These are my kind of people!" Borgian heard Bogstot shouting over the sound of the customers.

Borgian shoved his way past the crowds, remembering to look for the lionskin coat that this Aron was meant to be wearing.

Finally, Borgian saw someone who looked up to this appearance, wearing a lionskin coat, Borgian tapped on his back to an unexpected response.

The man suddenly tumbled back on to Borgian, another man had punched him.

"I'll have my coat back now, I think," the man that had given the punch, took the coat off the man that had crushed Borgian.

Borgian rolled the man off him to see the bearer of the coat's hand stretched out.

"Got to watch out for these drunks, they'll steal your coat and then fall on you ... or another, Aron's the name."

"Borgian," Borgian announced plainly.

"Ah, the one I'm meant to be meeting, good to meet you."

"Who the bloody 'ell are you!?" Bogstot came out of nowhere, very drunk, somehow, so quickly.

"A friend of yours?" Aron asked in a voice that sounded like he hoped not to have to deal with Bogstot.

"More or less," Borgian replied, "Lord Aron Amateir, meet Lord Bogstot Clairn"

"Lord!" Aron exclaimed, shocked, "I mean nice to meet you."

Aron extended a hand to shake but Bogstot started ranting instead, ignorant to the hand, "You are a strange man, where's your beard? Where do you come from?" Bogstot took a seat, it collapsed under his weight.

"Never mind, he'll be fine, now, down to business, we need your help with Tourjest."

"I'm already aware of our quest, have set a course too, a carriage outside awaits our arrival, we head to the elven city in the Benedoecs, Raschel Oki Frindal, we have nought information about the danger that lies within, my father was brief on the location of Tourjest Cavern too to further our lack of information. In the city lies the Chantry, a place where almost all information in Askaria lies, on ink and paper," Aron finished.

"So, you believe the elves will give up their knowledge willingly?" Borgian questioned.

"Of course not, but whatever the elves want in return shouldn't be as much a problem as journeying through no man's land, not knowing what we search for," Aron replied.

Aron hauled the unconscious, with alcohol, Bogstot, over his shoulder.

"We should head off right away, the carriage master won't take well to anymore waiting," Aron suggested, "have you said your farewells to the kind lady upstairs."

"Yes, let's go."

CHAPTER 19
THE SPARK WITHIN

"Water?" Frienz offered to his mother, Zensi Alok, a leather pouch, she took it without hesitation and drank till the last drop.

Zensi had large bags under her eyes and she looked as thin as a stick, her and Frienz had been wandering the roads and following the signs a long time now, barely surviving, trying to find their way back to Mezal city.

On the way, hoping to gather up their loyalists and take back Mezal from Mazdol, they still had the survivors from the Talgrin city Prison break-in and breakout, but they wouldn't be enough.

Zensi felt weak and it wasn't just because she hadn't eaten for a day or had just received her first drink since the prison, it was really because she was without Georlia, the blind woman, her loyal stewardess, who had guided her through her life since the death of her father by Mazdol's hand.

"She'll be okay, Georlia, we'll find her one way or another, take her back, we will undo Mazdol's evil," Frienz knew his mother's concern, he tried to comfort her, he put his hand on her shoulder, she shook it off.

"I don't deserve pity," Zensi bowed her head, "all my life, without knowing, I've been following in Mazdol's footsteps, becoming susceptible to power lust and the spoils of war, I have ignored you your whole life, even turning your love to bait, I used your love to capture and interrogate Mazdol's daughter, I destroyed your love."

Frienz was shocked by the truth, his love for Ariesa, she had tried to extinguish as Mazdol had.

"You don't even have a father, I created you from my fear, created you from arcane magic input in my womb, no man, I have ever allowed to touch my heart, so I birthed you just as an heir and nothing else, no child should grow up without a father or with a mother who was never there," a single tear rolled down her cheek, she wiped it and stood a little taller, "Come on, we must journey forth, in my prophecy, I saw the crown yearning for a male figure, perhaps Mazdol, but Arch King or city lord, Mazdol will never rule over my family, my people, my city, the crown is not his yet, and whilst he doesn't control me, we will rebel on, to kill him."

CHAPTER 20
ONAFEL KRICAEIN FRINDAL

"Halt, passage to Raschel Oki Frindal is forbidden to the children of Bersi Koli Nare."

After long through the orange coloured forests and elegant, emerald plains, they had reached Raschel Oki Frindal, translated to 'City of Prosper'.

A large barricade of elven guards in pristine, shimmering golden armour and breastplates were blocking the entrance and denying passage through to the city.

"It was a bad idea in the firs' place, let's go back or would someone kindly explain what in the six boroughs is a Bersi Koli Nare?!" Bogstot shouted, pale-faced and looking ill in his hangover.

"Bersi Koli Nare is the elven god creator of the human species, happy," Aron explained.

Bogstot made a grunting sound, "'Ell, are you gonna do somet'ing," Bogstot glanced at Borgian.

Borgian then fluently spoke to the elves, "Ewi exile norkae o Malice oki Snowe, ensi quiol to norkae e uiq yul knowrei."

"In the name of all dead hope," Aron exclaimed in awe.

"Where did yeh learn tha'," Bogstot asked, staring at the elves hurrying to open the city doors.

"You find you have a lot of spare time on your hands in an elven prison," Borgian grinned smugly.

"Raschel Oki Frindal awaits you, sons of Bersi Koli Nare, may you Frindal as the great city hath."

The elves bid them entrance and as the doors opened, a glorious sight treated their eyes; colossal, marble buildings, cobblestone paths freckled with gold, houses stretching over to each other— creating bridge-like structures and gardens larger than the actual houses, full of every type of flower, painting every colour imaginable.

Borgian noticed the cool shade and as he looked up to see what blocked the sun, he caught sight of the sky forest.

Hung up in the air, were plenty of every type of tree; spruce, acacia, willow, holly, cherry, oak, all there, with athletic elves swinging from vine to vine for their own, and other's amusement.

Suddenly, they came to a halt, and Borgian's movement faltered with the sound of the others' footsteps fading.

A building shaped like a semi-sphere poked out of the ground, it was made from a material recognised by Borgian, as orichalcum, and was embroiled with many gems and crystal geodes.

Plated in gold, above two moon white doors, into the location, were the words:

Tei Chantrye: Onafel Kricaein Frindal

Suddenly, the ground shook, a cold breeze swept over the city and at the same time, it swept over the whole of the land.

A voice rang out, "You are like my brother, Borgian, a trying idiot, history is repeating itself but this time, everyone will die, you will fail."

The voice was gone, Bogstot and Aron were staring at Borgian in confusion.

"We don't have much time," Borgian whispered.

They proceeded down into the depths of the Chantry, they opened the nearest door and went on forth, the room was lit by eerie green lamps and in the back of the room, his skin, like an emerald snake's in the light of the lamps, was the High Elv Senator of Knowledge and Secrets, Civiarin.

"Aron and Bogstot, I never thought to see your faces again, how the years have been cruel … but a new face, Borgian Steel, come to sell your soul for some piece of knowledge," Civiarin laughed cruelly.

"Sorry to break it to you but I have no soul to sell, I lost it to an undead elven knight and king, and my name? I'm always surprised by how people seem to know it," Borgian voiced.

"High ranking bandit turned homeless traveller in search of a long-lost artefact thought to have never existed, and the Malice of Snow, you started it and now you want to end it, hilarious … easy regrets, hmm," Civiarin smiled, "that's how you lost your soul, isn't it, and you're here for information on how to get it back."

"And to save Askaria."

"Yes, whatever, so, I am supposing you wish to know the origins of the blade, yes, Ethril I believe? A good story that one, a piece of vital history to the southern lands away from Askaria," Civiarin began searching through a shelf full of books, now visible in the green lamp Civiarin carried with him, he revealed a dark red book, the colour of blood with gold lettering engraved:

'Forgotten Legends: The Curse of Bolgron Island'

"The price of my knowledge into your hands, I wish for you to fulfil any deed I ask of you in the future, and you will fulfil it otherwise you will find yourself eating Bogstot's tongue or your own if he dies before the necessary time," Civiarin indicated to Borgian.

Civiarin sat on what looked like a leather-covered throne, stood on the other side of the room.

He began to tell the story.

"It was on Bolgron Island where the King Rolgirtis, his brother, Gothrog and all inhabitants of the great elven cities there, heard the voice of the evil Dycrite lord, Sycron who wished to take over their land for his own, of course, the White Elves refused and so

Sycron spun his curse," Civiarin paused and flicked through the pages, skipping parts that he obviously thought were not vital, "after a great journey, the two brothers found a grand forge to a name forgotten, where, with legendary materials, the Sword of Fading was forged, a weapon powerful enough to challenge a god which is what Rolgirtis did, he brought the Malice of Snow to a halt but soon, with the presence of the sword, Rolgirtis became corrupted, he became a tyrant, a slave master, putting his whole, already scarce in numbers, species of White Elves to work and executing those who refused or went even a little below his expectations.

Next, Rolgirtis commanded of his slaves, the creation of a new blade, and they fulfilled it but instead of delivering it to their king, they delivered it to Gothrog who vowed to free them from their bounds and he kept to his promise, Rolgirtis was defeated but with his defeat, the island was ravaged with an uncontrollable after effect of the curse, slowly killing every man, woman and child of the White Elv species.

Gothrog took his brother with him to Askaria where he left the knowledge of a white book and the legend of the blades with the first human he found who turned out to be the ancestral founder of Clan Amateir, and Rolgirtis—now a frozen figure due to his defeat—was hidden along with Gothrog himself who did so in the knowledge that he himself would become corrupted too, eventually" Civiarin finished.

"But where is Tourjest? Where's 'e hid," Bogstot inquired.

"Tourjest, the rumoured cavern? Yes, yes, I know where that is but that will also cost you," Civiarin showed his teeth, like pearls, in his grin.

"Fine, Civiarin but I'm only putting down the traditional price on this," Borgian announced, "500 Heads."

"You must be kidding, 1000!" Civiarin pushed the price.

"Where do you stand to say that, elv?" Aron Amateir inquired.

"How dare you, I am High Senator of Elven Knowledge and previous Secondary Lord of the Senate of Mirrorlare."

"Previous?" Aron laughed purely to annoy Civiarin, "Okay, elv, how about this, Borgian will pay the 500 Heads and I will give you this."

Aron reached into his belt pouch and revealed a small silver dolphin token.

"A family heirloom from the second age," Aron handed it over to Civiarin who snatched it up quickly, examining it with intense curiosity.

"We have a deal."

"Are you sure you want to do this?" Borgian questioned, feeling guilty.

"Yes," Aron reassured Borgian, "now hand over the Heads."

Borgian reached into a pouch on the internal side of his bearskin cape and revealed five blood-red coins with the number '100' stamped on each one, he passed them to Civiarin begrudgingly.

"The furthest west of Askaria, then walk slightly south until you reach a steep cliff face, you know what to do next, Amateir," Civiarin gave the directions to Tourjest as he pocketed the coins and the heirloom.

"Oh, and one more thing, Borgian, don't forget, anything I request."

Again, the sound of wheels turning stone and dirt upwards, and that of the horses whinnying as the carriage turned a corner.

Aron steered the carriage, using the crop to control the steeds.

"How valuable was that heirloom?" Borgian asked Aron, worried.

"It wasn't worth anything, it was a fake, my father has the real one, he would have never trusted me with the real one and apparently, for good reason."

Borgian breathed a sigh of relief, "Wait, how did Civiarin not notice?"

"Elves hate to admit it, but they ascended from sprites who were pretty much blind, either that or they are just too arrogant to see."

"Very arrogant," Bogstot mumbled.

"Night has fallen, are we even close to Tourjest?"

"Open your eyes, Borgian," Aron set the carriage to a halt and pointed to the cliff face that Civiarin had talked about.

They all dismounted and walked towards the rocky, rough cliff.

Aron placed his hands on a spot and muttered: "Rite of passage, rite of blood."

Before Borgian could blink, the wall was gone, and a narrow passageway lay before them, they entered inside and the view at the end of the path that lay before them, was like something from a fairy tale.

An amphitheatre-like stone building with beautiful, superior structures of dark, yet beautiful, ice decorating its walls took up most of the huge cavern it was encased in.

At the centre of the strange, alien formation of stone and ice, was a sword of blue silvery material, the Ethril Blade.

They entered through the top and passed down through dark corridors that circled and dropped.

Soon enough, the three men had arrived at the bottom where the blade perched on a granite slab.

"The Ethril Blade…"

CHAPTER 21

THE ONE THEY CALL THE COAL KING

They practically ran, despite their exhaustion and unforgiving fatigue that soon did, eventually, bring them back to walking pace.

"What could have built this?"

Aron's question was not answered.

Bogstot and Borgian looked on in awe at the walls surrounding them, they were inscribed with detailed sculptures of the story of Gothrog and Rolgirtis.

Finally, they came across the corridor holding the entrance to the blade's chamber.

They continued to the blade, it was so close now but then...

Smash!

A huge gate, previously open, closed shut.

All three of them pushed against the gate at once, nothing.

Bogstot went red in the face, "Blasted, cursed door!"

He spat on the ground.

Borgian looked for something that could help them, and after a half an hour, giving up, he leant back against a wall, it felt very uneven, strangely so.

Borgian turned around to see the wall, there were pictures inscribed on the wall, similar to the previous walls: it showed a gate made from ice and a torch edging near it, on another wall, it showed the gate on fire and the next, the gate was gone.

"Do you have a torch somewhere?" Borgian looked to Aron.

"Yeah, it's not lit though."

"I've got some flint and steel, don't worry about it," Borgian retrieved the torch from Aron and lit up the torch with the sparks of the flint.

Borgian moved the torch towards the gate and as the light shined on the gate, the gate seemed to transmute into ice.

Borgian touched it, it was real, he took out his sword, Slayer, and smashed it against the gate.

The gates broke, shattering into a thousand frozen pieces.

"How the bloody 'ell…"

Borgian continued to smash the gate until, but the broken shell of the frame remained.

Aron and Bogstot stood up to join Borgian.

They progressed on.

Borgian breathed a sigh, "Let's get this over with."

Borgian felt a chill, he shivered.

"Take up the sword, finish what you began," the eerie voice echoed through the cavern.

Disheartened, Borgian looked at the two men behind him for reassurance.

They nodded.

"Know, spirit, creature, whatever form you lie in. I do this of my own will, no one commands me, I challenge my blade to yours."

Borgian took a deep breath and at exhalation, placed his hands on the blade's handle, it was cold like the ice skimming the cavern and its structure, and then suddenly a blue light emitted from Borgian's hand and meshed with the blade.

A screeching sound suddenly sounded from below, the area they were on vibrated, the structures of ice around them began to crash to the ground, smashing like glass.

Borgian was losing his balance.

Then, the floor collapsed below them.

They were falling fast into the darkness below.

Borgian tried to hold onto the Ethril Blade as best as he could but with the fall becoming tighter and the walls closing in so that his shoulders became bloody and bruised, he let go as he crashed down into the ground below, he was saved by the softness of the layers of moss growing over it.

Thank the gods.

The structures of ice started to fall in and had to be dodged.

The screeching began again, much louder.

The Ethril Blade started to tremble violently, Borgian could scarcely see as a hulking black figure with glowing blue eyes and a frosty coating skimming its body, appeared.

Everyone was silent, the Ethril Blade suddenly lit up the place with a blue glow and it, he, was revealed: Gothrog the Coal King.

A horrible sound, like the scraping of a chalkboard, left the thing's mouth.

Borgian, Bogstot and Aron ran through the darkness into a place covered with ancient ruin, hoping it would aid them in obstructing Gothrog's pursuit.

Unfortunately, it wasn't enough.

He smashed his giant, coal fists into the ruins and the walls of the pit, shattering the already crumbling rock.

The trio were vulnerable to his blows.

They ran even faster, in fear, constantly looking behind themselves, they struggled for breath and the cold air felt like daggers in their lungs.

Borgian felt he couldn't run much longer, and then he saw it, a crack in the wall, it was small, but perhaps, still big enough to take in a person.

Risking his chances, he quickly slipped in.

Borgian felt a little of his skin scrape and tear as he entered in, he stepped back, he saw Gothrog approaching fast before he fell, down he went once more.

He had fallen into an underlayer of the vast pit, with two large tunnels, one on either side of the cavern.

It was lit up by the sunlight coming through one of them, the other— a roar echoed through.

Gothrog was still coming, Borgian decided to hide behind a large rock.

Firstly, Bogstot and Aron came through the tunnel, followed by Gothrog, Borgian jumped out at the opportune moment, blade in hand, he drove it into the thing's back, it screeched in agony, writhing in pain, reaching for its back with its gnarled, inhuman arms.

Borgian let go as Gothrog fell back, the beast tried to scuttle onto its front like a beetle but soon fell still, it's carcass was now being consumed by ice, spreading from the wound made by the Ethril Blade, before Gothrog was fully consumed, he let out plumes of black smoke from his body and then...

He was dead.

Borgian inhaled, the fumes entered his nostrils, his throat tightened, the two anxious faces of his companions were the last things he saw before entering the dark.

"Borgian Steel," Borgian opened his eyes, he was in what looked like a marble temple.

"Welcome to the Pearl Palace, I believe you've been here before recently, for me—it's been a while, I'm glad to be back here after so long. You freed me, Borgian, this is my resting place," A tall snow-white-skinned elv with large ears, greyish blue eyes and white hair: Gothrog, exclaimed.

"What do I do next, how do I find your brother, and defeat him?" Borgian questioned.

"To defeat him, all you need to do is use that blade, your soul has merged with the Ethril Blade and now has meshed with the sword, you bear its powers, and now a piece of your soul lies in both blades and yourself … you won't need to find him, he'll find you but, in any case, to return the favour, look down at the blade."

Borgian did, a snow-coated Mezal city was what he saw, not his reflection but Mezal city and the Malice of Snow.

CHAPTER 22
FOLLOWING WINTER

Borgian sat upright, Aron had been filtering water into Borgian's mouth using a hollow bamboo staff, they were sitting next to a pond in the shade of the trees outside of the tunnel exit Borgian had seen from inside Tourjest.

In the corner, leaning against the tree, Bogstot was sharpening his weapons.

"I saw it…" Borgian started to wheeze, he was short of breath, "it's … coming," Borgian was fading out again, he closed his eyes, but he was slapped by Bogstot who had got up now, "what's coming?"

"Malice … Mezal city … we need to go."

Borgian forced himself up, he collected his cape and checked that the internal bag on the cape contained all his possessions, it did.

He then took up the Ethril Blade which had previously been sitting on a tree stump, he looked at one of the sides of the blade, the image of Mezal city had got clearer since his blackout, dream meeting with Gothrog.

Borgian secured the blade in the sheath that had once held his faithful sword, Slayer, he noticed slayer was now in a saddlebag on one of the horses of three, tethered to a nearby oak.

Borgian noticed they were straining their muscles and digging their hooves into the ground, they were trying to run, to get away.

The horses' eyes pleaded with Borgian, they were large and staring.

"Do you think animals respond to the Malice of Snow, do you think they know when it's coming?" Borgian asked, looking at the creatures who looked like they had seen ghosts.

131

"We were going to ask you the same question, one minute they were waiting outside the cavern exit, patient and still, like soldiers, the next, they tear the ropes restraining them and are off, running like the wind, they all went off in separate directions and tore the carriage to shreds."

Borgian noticed the ruined carriage in the background.

"We just followed them to here and they were alright ... until now," Aron explained, eyeing the fearful animals.

"Well, let us help these beasts out as they help us in return, best to be off now and arrive at Mezal before this blasted, cursed weather," Borgian jumped onto his steed as he stated his decision.

Bogstot nodded his head and looked at Aron, "He's right, we better be off."

"I know," Aron responded with gritted teeth, he had not come to appreciate Bogstot's character.

Bogstot and Aron both mounted their horses: Aron smoothly. Bogstot with trouble, his saddle, specially fit to adapt to his weight, was unfortunately not available.

Borgian asked Aron. "How long will you continue with us on this quest, when do you head back home."

"Soon" Aron looked up to the sky and smiled, "when Mezal is safe, I will head back home, to Amateir City, to the Sundered Isles, where the air is free and carries the scent of salt, where the food is crisp and fresh and the women," he took a breath, pulling a longing face "As pretty as they come..."

"I knew a friend who would disagree with you, always the Sesan women when it came to him..."

"Too bad Sesan is now but a heap of debris and un-melting frost."

"Enough talk, last time I checked, Mezal wasn' Malice of Snow proof," Bogstot put forth.

Borgian took out the Ethril Blade from his sheath and turned around to swiftly cut the ropes that kept the unhappy steeds at bay.

Without having to even lay hands on the reigns, the horses were off, as fast, or from the rider's point of view, even faster than lightning.

Borgian managed to keep his horse to a controllable pace and with the wind whistling in his ears, he felt the unmistakable cold.

To every side of him, he soon saw it fall, the snow.

It was about to start.

The Malice of Snow was about to arrive.

"Quick, get down, into the bushes, now's our chance," Zensi whispered.

Frienz obeyed and they both crouched down, out of sight, into an emerald green shrubbery as a horde of well-armoured warriors bearing the black boar and dagger of Clan Herginn, came around the corner.

Zensi and Frienz silently loaded the two pipes that had been roughly carved from the branch of tall dead oak they had encountered earlier on during their journey, with darts.

They blew on their pipes and hit a couple of unsuspecting soldiers and as the poison from the darts entered their brains, they unleashed their arsenal on the helpless, confused soldiers who had not been hit with poison, they were hacked to death in spurts of blood and separation of limbs before the two hit with poison, detached their chest plates, brought their weapons to their own chests and dragged down to their bellies, ripping the barriers of skin that had previously kept the entrails that soon spilt over the floor ... all the Herginn warriors were dead.

"Rather gruesome but very efficient. What poison did you use?" Zensi questioned her resourceful son.

"Bloodbeetle venom, not the kindest neuropathic agent, tells the brain to eliminate any major life force in the area, including their own."

Zensi nodded in understanding before rushing to the scene.

"Lucky, the two poisoned soldiers removed their armours, otherwise the blood would have given us away, come take one," Zensi beckoned to her son.

Frienz strapped one to his shoulders, "Heavy," Frienz exclaimed.

Frienz bent down to recover the boots from the dead soldiers, he found a piece of parchment within.

"Mother, look at this."

Frienz passed the parchment to his mother who read it eagerly:

In fond hopes that this finds you well, Z & F,

This message comes from Mezal, you know who sends this, I have received your letter and have heard about Georlia, I now understand it is time for me to show you something.

Also, send the courier back as soon as possible if alive, if dead, take his disguise, it should serve as a key to the city, he will try to misguide a group of Herginn soldiers into nearing locations where you could possibly be, so kill one of the soldiers too for the other armour,

A-

"He was one of us," Zensi realised.

"Who was he."

"A loyalist, he served his purpose, let us not dwell on his lost life, he is with the Edicryte now" Zensi went quiet for a few seconds to show respect for the lost soul, "with this armour, it should be easy to gain passage into Mezal, where we plan to go anyway, Georlia may have to wait."

"Are you sure?" Frienz asked his mother.

Zensi nodded in reply, fighting back tears, worried that if she talked, she'd burst out crying.

"And who are we looking for when inside Mezal?"

Zensi was sure Frienz knew who they were going to, perhaps he was just trying to change the subject.

"A: Aelius."

"Mazdol's grip shall falter, for Clan Alok," Frienz called out.

"For Clan Alok."

The whip struck her face again, it was sore, now, and dripping with blood.

She could only predict when the whip would smack down again, opening another of the many wounds on her face.

Georlia knelt, posed in place, she could sense the iron cuffs around her wrists, they were cold, the first time they were put on her, now they were warm with her oozing blood.

Through what Georlia thought was a dungeon, she could hear the jailkeeper's mutterings echo.

After trying to escape with her masters or her friends or her family, as they may be called, she was moved to Mezal so Mazdol could keep a closer eye on her.

He was fuming that Zensi had escaped and ever since, he had been torturing and intimidating Georlia.

A sallow voice sounded in Georlia's direction, "Mazdol has requested you for dinner, he wishes to know what you want to eat," It was the voice of the head jailor, Mogron Redthorn.

Georlia would not answer to such a cruel person made the head of something by Herginn, but she soon changed her mind after hearing the noise of iron grinding against the wall suddenly.

"I'll ask one more time, what do you want for dinner."

"Garlic and sandfish soup," Georlia quickly said, it was a meal she had once shared with a family of fishermen before the days of serving the Alok family.

She listened, the sound of footsteps retreating from the room.

She was alone and would have liked to stay like this forever rather than have the torturers come back.

She feared Mazdol, there were things she had seen Mazdol do and things she had seen he would do, to save Zensi the stress, she would never tell her.

As much as Georlia hated to admit it, Mazdol was a good leader, with his ruthless nature, his well-placed paranoia and his rightly forged alliances, but the things he had done and would do would change who he really was completely.

The ground was now blanketed with white, the snowfall had got heavier and heavier.

A muddle of eerie voices seemed to protrude from the evil, white, icy mist.

"Once, we could not see, but the ice froze our eyes open and now we can see," a woman's voice exclaimed.

"But we were scared and we rebelled against the great Sycron for our land, we dishonoured knowledge and made a blade, so," a man's voice continued, "to see how we had corrupted goodness and forged the blade, made our benevolent protector leave us but at least now, the evil one could not touch us due to the blade, our corrupted king enslaved us but his brother set us free with another great blade, but we were still diseased, left for dead, and so we became the Disavowed, by gods and kings."

Borgian wished for the voices to stop, Aron and Bogstot obviously did too, their faces showed fear, the horses sped off even faster.

"The sea was frozen, our food was ravaged by plague, we were deprived and as we faded in our mutated forms, we became part of the blade, a figment to be unleashed once more," Borgian could see Mezal city up ahead as the story climaxed to an end, "now we return, feel the pain that we once did," the Malice of Snow could be seen clearly now, trees froze blue before it, the gathering wave of destruction through ice and snow, "Rolgirtis controls us once again but our allegiance is true only, to the great and terrible winter and snow."

"Ah, we meet again, Georlia, previous stewardess of Mezal city. Please take a seat, enjoy the meal," Mazdol signalled to the seat at the end of the table or at least Georlia thought he did, she couldn't see.

She felt for some object and came across a large, rough wooden surface, she continued doing this until she came across a gap and then a smooth wooden surface, the chair.

She stumbled onto her seat and took a stressed breath, she smelled the meal, she picked up the punchy scent of strong cheddars, the whiffs of chicken and pork and then the salty aroma as she recognised the garlic and sandfish soup, it was alluring, it was hard to resist, if feasting with the Aloks, she would have tucked in straight away but she feared poison, then again why would Mazdol poison her if he no-doubtingly wanted something...

She hesitantly took a bite of the pork, it was peppered with rosemary and salt, delicious.

She could hear the crackling of the fire and suspected that she was in a room made of stone due to the cold and the echo Mazdol's voice had made.

The only sound in the room now must have been Georlia's chewing, Mazdol stayed quiet and although Georlia could not see it, the tyrant's eyes were fixed on her intently.

Georlia let this continue for a few more minutes, she couldn't stop eating until she was finally full.

"Not hungry anymore, hmm?" Mazdol questioned, Georlia could smell his breath, it smelt heavily of beer which surprised her.

"I am elderly, I am blind but what makes you think this pleasuring will make me fall to your biddings, I have little to offer you, I have no idea where Frienz and Zensi are and I have no secrets to lend," Georlia stopped, trying to come up with something else to say, "and I use the word 'pleasuring' loosely, the torturing part brought me no happiness" she finally croaked.

"Oh, my dear woman, I believe you do not know where the Aloks lie, I do not want that information... I want you to consider my future, Zensi has had her turn, many times over and over, I will provide you with the necessary ingredients and—"

"I need no ingredients, my lady, Kinsia, provides them for me," Georlia interrupted Mazdol, "but what will you give me in return, my freedom?"

"Perhaps, I'll consider it."

This was not a good enough answer for Georlia, "My freedom," Georlia wasn't asking now.

"I'll remind you you're are in no position to ask anything of me," Mazdol announced begrudgingly, "but I believe we have an agreement."

Georlia nodded her head and then parted from her seat, raising her head to the ceiling, she muttered a silent prayer, whispered the words of the sacred rite and for a few seconds, she felt concealed, she felt safe, protected by her goddess, Kinsia.

She then forgot that she was considering the future of Mazdol and started accidentally looking into her own: she could see Mezal city, she zoomed into the tallest tower, saw Mazdol exit the tower, red-faced, she saw herself left there, and a second later, her vision became clouded by snow and when it re-adjusted, the top of the tower was gone.

She felt fear and her vision soon became something of a nightmare, she saw herself at the top of the tower and she couldn't stop herself, she jumped.

The vision ended suddenly, and paranoia struck her.

"What did you see?" Mazdol asked slightly worried, he could see the expression on Georlia's face.

Georlia stared for a few seconds, processing, before finally shouting, "We need to go now, please, Mazdol, the Malice of Snow is coming, we need to get out of here," Georlia suddenly started feeling for a door, and when she found something with a doorknob, she threw all her weight against it, it was no use and no sooner than then, had Mazdol pulled her away from the door and sat her down again.

She was suddenly encumbered by exhaustion and terror, she couldn't move, she was paralysed with fear.

CHAPTER 23
THE FALL

"Do you hear something?" Zensi looked at her son.

"Yes, I do, what is it?" Frienz exclaimed.

They were both dressed in layers of steel and clunky chainmail painted with Herginn red.

Both of them looked around, as it came, a mass of humongous clouds as high as mountains, rolled in, the Malice of Snow in its avalanche-like form.

The two ran as fast as they could, the armour was becoming a major problem at this moment, holding them back, their run was more like a fast walk in this state.

They began to sweat, and each drip froze on their skin.

Frienz and Zensi were considering taking off their armour at this point.

It was coming closer and closer and closer...

They both stopped, not because they had given up but because they literally couldn't move, their feet were frozen to the ground.

...But then their hope was regained, from out of the snowy mist came three figures on horseback.

Borgian, Bogstot and the last, she could not fathom who he was.

Zensi removed her helmet so that she could be recognised.

Borgian jumped off his horse quickly and smashed the frost holding their feet to the floor, "Get on!"

Borgian remounted his steed and Zensi jumped on his, Frienz accompanied Bogstot.

They went on, towards the city.

"I said tell me my future! Old crone, I swear I will pull your head from its roots if you do not give me what I want!" Mazdol was frustrated.

"Are you a complete idiot, do you not understand. We are all going to die!" Georlia tried to force sense into Mazdol, "take action now and you can save this city."

Georlia could sense Mazdol's anger now, that his face was alight with rage and frustration.

Georlia heard it then, the sound of sword from sheath, steel from leather.

Georlia had only heard of this blade once, usually, Mazdol used an axe known as Myrmidon, Georlia had heard this blade was named Cav'zafar, dragon tongue for executioner...

Suddenly then, the door swung open, Georlia could hear the squeak of the hinges and the harsh voice of a soldier sounded, "Lord Herginn, the Malice of Snow lies at our gates ... it has arrived, a pilgrim on his way here from Westgard reports that he saw shadows of disgusting, giant creatures walking through the snow."

"I told you and you did nothing, you are nothing but too late now," Georlia mocked, giving a smirk.

Mazdol sheathed his weapon and gave a command, "Gather all the townspeople and send them to the Temple of Liathin, it should hold against the minor forces of the snow, then gather the men and prepare to defeat whatever lies within, we just have to hope that Borgian returns soon with a solution to all this."

Georlia heard the soldier leave.

"And as for you, you will stay here, under lock and key until this is over, I want you present and alive for what I will do to you," Mazdol exclaimed cruelly.

Georlia stayed quiet, she felt the movement of the cold air as Mazdol passed and heard the clicking of the door as it locked shut.

Georlia began to get teary, she could not endure any more torture, she would have been glad for Mazdol to have had ended it then ... but then she remembered, her prophecy, she wouldn't be alive to be tortured again but she couldn't let herself die by slowly being frozen either, she would go out on her own terms.

There was never a corpse at the top of the ruins of the tower and she knew why.

Georlia stood up and grabbed the chair, she moved it around with her, it screeched on the wooden floor, as she felt the walls for something else useful—she could feel the silk of banners, the frames of portraits and the smooth wooden shelves bearing heavy hardback books—but then she found it, the feeling of glass at her fingertips, her future was so obvious now, she knew what to do.

She picked up the chair holding it up above ground, and with all the strength she could muster, she slammed it into the glass window, it broke easily.

She heard the smash and she could hear the howling winds that brought snow on them, and entered the tower room.

The door opened behind her and as she climbed into the empty window frame, the soldiers urged her to stop but she knew that what she was about to do was better than facing Mazdol's wrath and the pain that he would inflict upon her.

Would this be her last moment, she couldn't tell but she had an idea, her brittle bones, but she didn't want to dwell on that right now.

She inhaled, and she was there on that windowsill.

She exhaled, and she was gone.

CHAPTER 24
THE FORSAKEN

Zensi had seen her falling to the ground as soon as Borgian's horse reached the city.

Georlia; the godspeaker, the sear—suicide...

The soldiers were preoccupied and so the group managed to gain entrance easily into Mezal, Zensi re-equipped her helmet for disguise before jumping off Borgian's horse and running over to her old friend, Frienz followed her.

They both knelt by the dead sear's side as an old man Borgian recognised as Aelius ran towards them, he whispered something in Zensi's ear, she nodded, and they were off, Aelius caught sight of Borgian and came over quickly, "Remember the sword when the curse enters in, the Disavowed lie within. Good luck."

Frienz also looked over and gave an approving nod of thanks whilst he comforted his mother.

Borgian saw the Aloks and Aelius disappear through a sewage entrance, he saw Mazdol glancing in their direction too, Borgian hoped he hadn't realised who they were.

"Borgian! Borgian! Do you have the blade!" Mazdol suddenly rushed over to Borgian once he caught sight of him, Mazdol was followed by a small army of soldiers.

"Yes, I have it," Borgian replied.

"And you know how to use it?" Mazdol inquired.

"It's a bloody sword, what do you think!" Bogstot half-shouted.

"But there are many secrets to be revealed in battle and blood, I suspect," Mazdol admired the sword, "pretty thing, never seen a blade like it."

Mazdol turned to Georlia's body now, "Shame, oh well, she had her life, and she abandoned it ... abandoned it right out the window."

Mazdol's men sniggered.

"Have her head removed and her body burnt to ashes, somebody that disrespects the life the gods gave her, shouldn't have a proper burial."

Suddenly, many soldiers screamed, "They're in the snow!" and then were impaled by a giant of a creature, three times the size of Borgian, rags adorning their naked bodies, they had blue skin that looked rotten, dark blue eyes and sharp teeth like knives.

Where the hands should have been, they had spears of their own flesh.

It was exactly like the ones Borgian had seen at Bolgron Island.

Like the one that had killed Thalt.

The soldiers were ripped apart as the Disavowed tore them into ribbons, using the sharp nubs on the ends of their arms.

Borgian readied himself as more of the afflicted mounted the city walls and the huge wave of snow got ready to drop ... and then it did.

Large amounts of snow seeped through the city, painting it white and red.

A crunching sound made Borgian look around, across the city courtyard where mangled bodies lay with their bones sticking out in awkward, gruesome positions and others suffocated by the snow or crushed by its weight, lay dead—the top of the main longhouse tower which Georlia had jumped from, began to crumble.

Borgian made for an escape as the old, ancient bricks came tumbling down, killing more and more people.

Warm blood steamed on the snow.

The city had yet survived.

It was what came next that had the power to destroy Mezal...

The Disavowed had begun the killing, they did so fast.

Borgian looked at the sky to take in the sight, wondering if it would be his last, the sky was completely grey, a canvas in one shade speckled with white paint, the snow, if Borgian didn't have a promise to himself to keep, he would a mind to die with this beautiful yet dangerous scene.

"You have already lost," Borgian heard the icy voice disappear into the sky.

Suddenly, everything came into focus, the un-elves with their large mangled hands, grabbing unexpecting people and with horrible clicks, twisting the peoples' heads around so that it looked like they had always seen from that way.

The screams of those around, sounded.

Blood spilt, hot, on the snow.

Fear was abundant here.

Borgian readied his new blade, the Ethril Blade, as he heard the strange croak of one of the Disavowed's breathing, so with precision and a wish for luck, Borgian swung his blade back into something solid.

Borgian turned quickly to remove the Ethril Blade from its sheath in one of the Disavowed's skull and as he did, Borgian watched a spear of ice protrude from the wound in the Disavowed's head.

Aron then came out of nowhere and shouted at Borgian, "Keep that up, our weapons won't do anything," Aron struck a claymore, that he had prized from the hands of a soldier with a large gaping hole through his chest, into one of the creatures' back to no effect.

Aron watched as the claymore snapped across the thing's sticking-out spine, he held just the pommel in his hands.

He dropped it as he was pinned to the ground by the angered un-elv, he was being readied for a final blow.

Aron shut his eyes closed, waiting for his pass to the Elysium.

"Akrah," a strangled word came from the single Disavowed's mouth to the relief of Aron, he opened his eyes and Borgian had just removed the Ethril Blade from the tangles of the sinews of the Disavowed's neck.

Borgian helped Aron up quickly, "You need to find a safe place, get inside, there is nothing but death for fools here."

Aron nodded before retreating into the crowd.

Borgian ran into battle once more, killing many Disavowed as he went, spearing some in their faces with his blade as they tried to close in, Borgian found Mazdol and Bogstot fighting in the centre, failing.

Borgian slammed his blade down into an attacking Disavowed, it froze up into a transparent statue.

"Where the bloody 'ell 'ave you been, we've been 'aving our arses carved into bits whilst you've been fighting your own battles!" Bogstot yelled.

Borgian was too pre-occupied fighting the ensuing villains to reply to Bogstot's unhappiness.

"There's too many of them" Mazdol exclaimed as he leant for a weapon on the floor after his Cav'zafar broke into shards.

The group were outnumbered.

"Were all dead," thought Borgian aloud but then suddenly, the blade lit up in blue colour, all the Disavowed around started to disintegrate.

Borgian looked around to see the open gates of the city, shadows retreated into the faltering snow.

"Did we win?" One of the soldiers questioned.

A rumbling came from below them then, the ground began to quiver.

"Stay your positions," Mazdol ordered the remaining soldiers before realizing it was over, "we have won this battle, my friends!" Mazdol shouted out, "and although there will be more battles, we will win them too!"

Mazdol's soldiers cheered as Borgian looked through the fading snow, he saw the shadow of the one he feared, Rolgirtis the Blue Knight...

"You have won this time, but I warn you, on the first day of Cloudfall, we will meet each other on the battlefield, set at the Plains of the Patron near where the Seas of Pythres lap, you have ten days."

Borgian heard the telling well.

Askaria wasn't prepared.

CHAPTER 25
A RED MOON

"Ten days," Mazdol exclaimed under his breath.

He and Borgian stood, overlooking a balcony so high up on one of the longhouse towers, it felt like if either of them extended their arms, they could touch the heavens.

"Ten or so years ago, I would have thought the crown to be mine by now and yet all I have done in that time, is gained a shaky grasp on a half-destroyed city," Mazdol exhaled a warm breath that Borgian saw, like smoke in the night, "...and now it's as if I've just been given a death sentence and a date for the execution: the first of Cloudfall."

"The world is collapsing in on itself no doubt, Askaria risks utter destruction and all battles seem pointless but there may still be hope..."

"Get to the point, Steel," Mazdol edged Borgian onwards.

"I was born into a world of chaos, the old king Adermino already twenty-five years cold in his grave, a crown with no one's head to sit on, then, at my third Bannerhour, your father, Arcturus, dead and rumours that his son, you, planned revenge. All that even before you and Zensi started this stupid feud, and if that wasn't enough my home village burnt to ashes by wild witches and me taken by bandits, I would have thought this world to be gone before I reached even my tenth Bannerhour."

"Yes..."

"And yet Askaria and its people still live, scarred, yes, but alive, a miracle is this Askaria of today," Borgian finished.

"Miracles. They died when the Gods stopped looking down at us with at least a speck of acceptance, the old Godspeakers most likely only continue to retain their jobs because of the input of charity and respect they get from the religious nuts of Askaria," Borgian saw sorrow in Mazdol's face for the first time, "look at it all Borgian, the end of Askaria comes soon and we will all have wished the Veranthon Dynasty with their sorcery, armies and basilisks had killed our ancestors when they had the chance, when they were still alive, back thousands of years ago."

Borgian felt the weight of the Ethril Blade in its scabbard as he moved slightly, he looked down at the amazing piece of weaponry and thought.

"Send a letter to Raschel Oki Frindal, they hold the fastest and best of minds in Askaria, get them to study any material capable of what was seen today and get them to report back to us when they have found it, we need the right weaponry to—"

"My sirs, there is no need for that, I can help you," a well-built man who looked about in his mid-forties stood behind Mazdol and Borgian, "all I require is the blade to study on, by tomorrow's morn, I will have the material used to make the blade named and to where the material can be sourced from."

Mazdol raised an eyebrow suspiciously, "I don't believe I have met you, what is your name, and speak fast."

"Hymir Asger, I am a humble blacksmith and at your service."

Borgian passed the sword to Hymir, "You wouldn't believe me if I told you what I was up against to get this beauty, protect it with your life."

"Or you can expect your life to be taken in an even more painful way ... I haven't seen someone flayed in a long time," Mazdol told the blacksmith in a cruel, cold tone.

"Well you have my word, I'll be sure to bring back this blade in one piece," Hymir walked off with the blade, Borgian hoped he wasn't misplacing his trust in this stranger.

"You should take some rest, my friend," Mazdol opinionated, "you will live to see another day as many of this battle's attendants will not."

Borgian thought of something else to say but there was nothing.

He retreated back into the depths of the longhouse where he was met with the face of a rather tired looking Aron.

"Aron, is all alright."

"Yes, I just thought I'd let you know of my departure back to the Sundered Isles."

"A bit late in the night to head off, isn't it?" Borgian exclaimed.

"Yes, a little, but I need to head off now if I want to be back in time, I am to be overseeing the events of the Sacred Tournament, so must be off."

"It's been good having you on our journey, you have helped immensely, thank you."

"You are very welcome," Aron extended a hand and Borgian took it.

"Goodbye Borgian, I hope to see you soon, when all this has blown over."

"Come, it's not long around here."

"Care to tell us where we are headed, Aelius?" Frienz voiced.

"A safe place," Aelius replied in his mysterious, floaty tone of voice.

They sloshed through the sewers underneath the city, frequently viewing dead rats floating on top of the waste.

"Everything was so nicely planned out," Zensi exclaimed, "...but this blasted curse. We had the armour and everything."

"It was a nice thought, Zensi, but at this point, a try to take back your city would have been futile," Aelius announced.

"Then, why send the letter and the disguised courier."

"All I needed was for you to get inside the city, I said nought in the letter or in my own very words about a re-liberation," Aelius spoke, "I needed to show you something and I still intend to do that."

They walked on for a few seconds more in silence until Aelius halted.

To the right of them, carved into part of the brick sewer tunnel, was the symbol of the Kingbird and under it inscribed in dragon tongue: 'Blevsr arriy silv fouray'

Zensi recognised the saying even whilst it lay un-translated, it was the saying of her clan: 'Blessed are those with courage'.

Aelius moved to the wall and placed his mouth to it, he whispered a few words that went beyond Zensi's understanding of languages and in a rough shaking motion, the piece of wall removed itself from their paths.

"A long time ago when Mezal was constructed by your great ancestors, it was designed to consist of many secret catacombs running throughout its undergrounds, years later, rumours spread of a catacomb, this one to be precise," Aelius used his arm to present the place he talked about, the place they were in, "so to clear away this rumour, your ancestors built a sewer system beneath the city to ensure no one would find their true secret, a door was also installed, as you have just seen, to be especially safe. The knowledge to unlock the catacombs was only spread among Mezal's strongest allies."

"Why, only the allies, not the actual family of Alok?" Zensi questioned.

"Well, this may be strange for you to hear of all people, but members of your family were known to grant information to the Herginn family. Your aunt, Meylin Alok passed on information to Mazdol's father during the Battle of the Silver Spear which in the end, resulted in both of their deaths."

Zensi did not question that knowledge, she herself knew of Meylin's treachery, it was the reason her mother, Darle, had commit suicide, along with the stress of having to care for Zensi after her birth.

Zensi always felt responsible for the death of the mother she could not remember but knew, inside, it was truly Meylin's fault, her treachery and execution that led her mother to the end.

Once again, the trip stopped and out into the darkness, Aelius shouted, "Come forth Seekers, Clan Alok lives."

Suddenly, a vast amount of space became lit with torchlight, they could see now, it was like a huge cavern, like a whole hidden city in a massive cave.

They stared upon numerous small buildings, hundreds of wells and a vast population with many out, ploughing huge fields of neon yellows and dull greens, plants that Zensi had never stared upon before, lit up by emerald globes of floating light above.

Above all of this, on a raised piece of land, lay a large, majestic building surround by what looked like smaller versions of the largest one.

It was a magical sight to behold.

"Welcome to Harphia," Aelius smiled at Zensi and Frienz' bewildered yet amazed faces.

At that moment, a woman stepped out of the shadows and hugged Aelius, "Father, I am glad to see you got here safe ... with all of Herginn's guards around, I was worried you would be discovered on your way here."

"Ah, my dear daughter, Arntia, there was a distraction, the Malice of Snow unleashed its rage again and this time in our own Mezal city, I am glad to see you safe too, thank the Edicryte you were here whilst it took place," Aelius drank in the moment for a second, breathing a sigh of relief, "oh, and meet the Alok family."

Arntia paused a moment before giving a short bow and a respectful nod.

They began to walk further into Harphia.

"So, what exactly is this place?" Zensi inquired of Aelius.

"It's Mezal's backup plan, Harphia has been here longer than anyone today can remember and is home to the Guild of Seekers, a secret society sworn to help the Alok family to maintain glory and well, life."

Frienz and Zensi watched as a globe of light flew overhead and out of sight.

"The Seekers swear fealty and their very life to Clan Alok and theirs, I am a Seeker, but I prefer the ground level and a little sunlight now and again," Aelius chuckled.

"What are the globes of light?" Frienz questioned.

"None of us are really sure ourselves but—"

"But it helps the crops grow and gives us light," Aelius quickly finished Arntia's sentence, "it was most likely created by the Hall of Alchemists hundreds of years ago."

"Hall of Alchemists?" Frienz voiced.

"You'll find out all about that later, now if you would continue to follow me."

"How, how has all of this remained a secret?" Zensi wondered aloud.

Aelius shook his shoulders, "Years of precautions, counter-measures, secret entrances and exits, a bit of sorcery now and again ... It's impressive, is it not?"

"Yes, but why only tell us now of this hidden miracle?"

"Seekers, we are 'when times are dire', remember, I would have told you earlier when you still owned the city but the master kept me strictly to my oath, only to help when times are dire," Aelius

154

repeated the phrase again, "and now, yes, times are dire, when your enemies rule something of yours..." Aelius shivered a little, "very dire, but worry not, soon, you will sit your throne again and after that, the First Crown will sit you."

Zensi felt her hope rekindle within, she was relieved, perhaps there was a chance for Mezal, and her, yet.

Aelius opened a set of brass-handled doors before them.

"Now if you would enter in here, we have a city to reclaim."

Borgian stretched out his right arm, feeling the linens of the curtains shrouding the disappearing light reaching through the window.

Borgian couldn't go to sleep, not now, knowing that the Malice of Snow pushed on, hungry and wild, not now, knowing the Blue Knight was out there somewhere, plotting a great finale to this game he played over Askaria.

Borgian couldn't go to sleep.

Not now.

Borgian got out of bed, his bare feet, cold on the stone below, he walked across the room over to the door, he turned the handle out into the corridor and found himself at a window, he opened it and a refreshing, cold breeze swept over him as the moon rose and the sun downed.

Tonight's moon was red like an evil eye.

It cast an eerie scarlet light across the land, Borgian hadn't seen a red moon in a long time and he hated to look back on the last time he had seen it.

That was the night his village had been burnt to the ground by witches of the wild.

Borgian could remember the screams as they echoed through the night, Borgian was only just about four years old and on that night, fate had favoured Borgian, he had been out collecting water in a forest far away from his village, or perhaps not so much as he was captured by a bandit clan, the Tanlor camp, who had originally given him the name Gelly, a name for a girl meaning 'ugly one' until when he was old enough to confide in the marauders, he told them his story and his name was changed to Borgian meaning 'saved one'.

Borgian had had enough of the memories and decided to try to sleep again, he made himself become sleepy by counting the number of different voices he could hear, of people leaving their destroyed homes and the city.

The final numbers of voices he had heard before falling asleep was exactly one hundred.

Niemhe tried desperately, failing, to usher her son back to sleep after his nightmare, he was a six-year-old and she was his fifteen-year-old mother.

"God's above, why can't you sleep!" Niemhe shouted out in annoyance.

Her son, Michellio continued screaming, at least, Niemhe thought, it wasn't as bad as when he was swearing at her ('filthy slut' seemed to be his favourite phrase) or when he was biting her wrists.

Niemhe would have simply left her son in the room to cry himself to sleep if she had lived in a city, however, she instead lived in a village, Stone Mount, which was low on security and was attacked by wolves, giant asps, trolls, the living dead and creatures known as despairers that would follow you around all day, invisible, releasing a neurotoxin that brings the victim to remember every painful, upsetting moment of their life in vivid detail so that they end up on their knees, near insanity, begging for relief, which is when the despairer consumes its meal.

All of these creatures were attracted by sound and so Niemhe had to be careful with Michellio, otherwise she risked getting thrown out of the village, along with her son, legs and arms tied, for the wild to take them.

Suddenly, all at once, Michellio fell back into his straw pillow and started to snore, Niemhe breathed a sigh of relief and had to find the strength in her tired bones to walk across the house, which was one room, to her bed where the toilet, a hole in the ground, rested not far from.

After so many years, the stench didn't bother her anymore.

The only thing, she felt, that ever did properly bother her were the memories of her husband who had gone off hunting in the forest one night and had never come back.

She decided not to think about him, after all, she needed all the sleep she could get if she was going to be able to cope for the next few days of harvest approaching.

She nodded off...

And as she did, mist plumed around the village that night so that no person could see the horror-stricken event awaiting and as Niemhe dreamt of blood and death, trying to awaken from the nightmare, a child's scream pitched and then disappeared, Niemhe continued her nightmare, she saw the village collapse and the beasts enter in, and herself ... all alone.

Freezing in the mist.

CHAPTER 26
GODS

"We have arrived," Aelius announced, "the Hall of Alchemists."

The brass handled doors opened into a large brightly lit longhouse that remind her of her own, the hall was decorated with the greens of Clan Alok and a unique darkest green banner with the symbol of a white sun on it in the middle, the sigil of the Seekers.

The place was made from clay and wood and was adorned with two large stained-glass windows, staring from the front.

"This hall was believed to be where the Seekers' alchemists use to study ways of growing and stabilising nature underground without use of the sun, unfortunately the majority of their research is long forgotten although some suspect the globes of light, or sun crystals, were their creation," Aelius glanced at Frienz and Zensi to check for their consistent listening, "today, the hall serves as the longhouse of Harphia and home to the Seekers' inner circle."

They approached a new set of doors and before they entered, Aelius gave his respects, "I am deeply sorry about the Godspeaker."

"Don't be, it was suicide, Herginn broke her, he's the only person who needs to be and will be sorry for her," Zensi told.

"She deserves a proper funeral," Frienz suggested as Aelius was about to open the door.

"And how would we do that, Mazdol would protect her corpse and burn it himself just to mock me ... it's impossible."

"Nonsense, Madam, if the Godspeaker's funeral is your request, the Seekers would be happy to seek out and return her corpse to her owners for an honourable send-off, I can share your wish with your court, expect it fulfilled very soon," Aelius nodded at Zensi before opening the doors into the meeting room.

Zensi's first thought of it, was that it looked like a court that you would sentence people to death in, it was lined with stone chairs around the exterior: Aelius's chair was easily recognisable due to the braids of garlic that hung around it.

Aelius noticed some curiosity as they looked at his chair, "I once ventured up north to the Blue Mountains and may have accidentally entered the territories of many different vampire tribes, any place I've been in more than once where my scent can be traced, I find garlic useful, deadly to them, tasty to us," Aelius explained.

"Take your place at the Throne of Seekers," Aelius indicated to five stone chairs with melted gold finishes.

"Five chairs?" Frienz questioned.

"For Arch King Orphoenix Alok and his four children"

They all took their seats and almost instantly, the council of Seekers entered in to join them.

"Aelius, what are the meanings of these summonings."

"We have some guests, Chief Veirimen."

Veirimen was a tall, broad-shouldered man with a billowing dark grey and a black beard and a bald head, he wore a grey coat and weather-beaten features which made him look both superior and sinister yet friendly and certain too.

"Chief, meet Queen Zensi, our soon to be Arch Queen of Askaria and her noble son, Lord Frienz. Queen Zensi and Lord Frienz meet Chief Veirimen, leader of the Seekers and their operations, head of the secret council of Mezal and supreme lord and overseer of Harphia," Aelius introduced one another.

Veirimen bowed, "It is an honour to meet the family to which I and my council have dedicated our cause and very lives to."

Aelius smiled at the beginning of what he thought to be a new era, "So, shall we proceed with the meeting, it is time to decide the fate of the future."

Borgian Steel and Mazdol Herginn walked down the city's roads to the house to which they had been informed belonged to the man Borgian had entrusted the Ethril Blade to, Hymir Asger.

Along the path, Mazdol and Borgian talked.

"How is your feud with Zensi going?" Borgian asked hesitantly.

"Badly, I haven't heard of Zensi's movements since her escape from Talgrin, some of my men report seeing her in my soldiers' armour whilst in this city but the only evidence I have of that is a few dead soldiers, stripped nude along the way here … my fight is a frustrating one and it's worse now it's being played like a game of hide and seek," Mazdol gave a stressed, odd sigh.

"What have you found on this Hymir who I have lent my blade to?" Borgian questioned on a different subject.

"Nothing much, I've checked all of the records that this city has, even the ones that Zensi had drawn up before I took over, I only found out about this house by asking around, people say he moved in recently which may be why he doesn't have a citizenship record but that doesn't explain the fact his purchase of the house wasn't recorded, it's strange…"

Borgian looked around, the streets were partially in ruins, pretty much all houses, apart from the ones owned by people who couldn't afford it, were covered in scaffolding for reconstruction, and people lay sleeping on the pavement, waiting for their houses to be built.

"Stand out the way Borgian," Mazdol alerted quickly.

Borgian saw what Mazdol was talking about and stayed into the side as a scrawny beggar woman in the middle of the street retched up a mixture of blood and half-digested food onto the paving.

The woman's eyes rolled back into her head before she fell to the floor, her arms and legs twitched awkwardly for a while before she died.

Borgian opinionated, "We should finish the job, make sure she doesn't turn into one of—"

Suddenly a carriage came rushing down the street, the sound of bones breaking as it passed over the woman and disappeared around the corner.

"Well, that finishes the job, I doubt she'll be able to get up, Disavowed or not after that," Mazdol continued walking.

"How often does that happen?" Borgian heard the worry in his own voice.

"Enough for it to become a normality, but if you want a precise number, I can give you an average of about eleven deaths per day, it's usually always the poor, those that can't afford a remedy, not that a permanent cure has been found, none of us were expecting a virus to come out of the curse as well," Mazdol replied.

They soon came across an old, unstably made house with the golden anvil, the sign of the Blacksmiths League hung proudly above the door.

"This is the place," Mazdol announced.

"I had a hunch he was a blacksmith, but the Blacksmiths League, only the greatest smiths receive that honour, it looks as if there is more to this man than we thought."

"Yes, perhaps we entrusted the right man for the job, but I still wonder what else there is to him," Mazdol conversed.

Borgian walked to the door and knocked to no reply, once again he rapped on the door.

Nothing.

The next time he called out Hymir's name as well as banging on the door, still nothing.

Borgian stepped back and took a closer look at the house, he looked through the closed curtains of one of the windows, there was a gap that Borgian looked through.

"Shit," Borgian exclaimed.

"What is it?"

"The house is empty, no one's there," Borgian walked back to the door and slammed himself into it, the lock clicked, and the door flung open.

Borgian stepped into the house, there were shards of glass littering the floor, cobwebs in every corner and dust covering the bits of floor that weren't occupied by faeces

"It's not just empty, it hasn't even been occupied for whatever time causes bloody dust to gather and shit to turn solid," Borgian shouted as he shattered one of the faeces into shards of waste beneath his boot.

"Borgian, you may be wrong, look more carefully at the floor," Mazdol pointed out.

Borgian saw them now, footprints.

"Someone's been here recently," Borgian realised.

Mazdol nodded, "I'm going to get some soldiers to secure the place, you look for more clues, I'll be back," Mazdol left the house.

Borgian decided to follow the footprints, they didn't lead him far, after looking through two rooms, the trail had ended at the only thing intact in the house, a shelf bearing two single copper Heads and a miniature weighing scale.

Borgian looked at the scales he tried picking it up, but it was attached to the shelf somehow, he then looked at the two dusty, rusting Heads and then he wondered...

Borgian placed one coin on each scale, it balanced out almost perfectly.

Suddenly, part of the floor disappeared before Borgian, a set of stairs were revealed.

Borgian lit a torch and continued down the stairs with caution until he found a room, it was a shrine.

Before Borgian was an altar bearing sticky, drying blood, it wasn't just a shrine, it was a shrine to a Dycrite and on the altar, was more proof, a statue resembling a star, carved from obsidian, it was a shrine to Sycron, the Dycrite that Mazdol had heard the Disavowed reveal was the one that created the Malice of Snow.

Borgian inspected the room further, on the floor lay a book bearing a black star on its cover, the title read:

'The Tower of Night'

Borgian opened it and flicked through till a map fell out, it was a map of Askaria with a path from Mezal to the Tower of Night drawn on, Borgian pocketed it.

Borgian also inspected a passage that had been circled in the book:

'Those who wish to gain the favour of Lord Sycron must:

1.   Offer their services to him in life and death

2.   Travel on monthly pilgrimages to the Tower of Night

3.   Establish an altar to him

4.   Perform the monthly sacrifices

5.   Perform the Cleansing Ritual in which you must find an item to which you have been asked by Sycron to retrieve, and bring it to him to receive your new cleansed, great form'

Borgian reported all that he had found, back to Mazdol who waited outside with his soldiers on the street.

"So, he has the blade and is god knows how far on his journey already, I have no man stupid enough to take up a journey to Nevara's Pass so let's all just slit our throats now and be done with it."

"Mazdol, old friend, you forget who stands before you, I'm stupid enough to go, aren't I?"

"You're far from stupid Borgian ... are you sure you want to go? You understand that you will go alone and that the fate of Askaria will be on you."

"I will go, Mazdol, I accept whatever's coming to me."

Mazdol placed a hand on Borgian's shoulder, "Be careful, the mountains of Nevara's pass are extremely dangerous, more so when alone, and I am yet to see the tower atop the peaks and the dark power of the god that inhabits there—I cannot lose my best friend, not now, take care, gods be with you."

"Michellio!" Niemhe called, "Time to wake up!"

There was only silence.

"Michellio?" Niemhe walked over to her son's bed, still trying to fully open her tired eyelids.

She stared at the bed for a while, the blanket was flat, there was no sign of a body, just a bouquet of flowers tied together with yellow lace, she removed the blanket and stood there, paralysed for a minute.

Fear gripped her.

Her son was not there.

Niemhe stepped out of her house to a crowd of angry villagers.

"Your child was screaming outside of your house last night, he alerted the wolves!" one shouted.

"We thought we had told you to shut him up, no other child in the village causes such a ruckus, and why in hell would you let him out at night," an older villager called Rona commented.

"He was outside, screaming," Niemhe clapped her hands over her mouth and burst into tears, "where is my boy?"

The villagers then looked guilty to find out Michellio was missing and to not have told her sooner, of his appearance outside.

The villagers all shook their heads at each other to confirm none of them had seen the boy.

Suddenly, through the crowds, a small girl known as Mia burst out, "I saw them in a dream, the masked men with the snake staffs, they were bringing the boy to a big building place," Mia was a seven-year-old who always seemed to have these interesting dreams, she was plagued by them.

One of the adults ushered her down, "Go back home, Mia, us adults have to solve this."

"But—"

"Now."

With Mia's return home, the villagers began searching the village to no result, in the end, the villagers gave up and tried to continue their normal day.

Niemhe headed back to her house.

She felt her whole world collapse before her.

She had nothing now.

When Niemhe entered her house, she slumped into the only chair in her house and then noticed she had forgotten to close the door.

Suddenly, before she had time to get up from the chair, the door slammed closed.

The little girl, Mia, appeared from the place the door had hidden a moment ago.

"I'm not lying you know," she exclaimed.

Niemhe stayed silent.

"I don't know if you've noticed but every time something even a little bit strange happens, I have a weird dream that then turns out to become the next part of these strange things."

"Like an omen," Niemhe whispered under her breath, realising.

"A what?"

"A sign that has something to do with the future, if you are able to see omens, it means you have been gifted a great power from the Edicryte goddess of dreams and omens, Kinsia, to be able to see such things," Niemhe felt like what she was saying was a little bit farfetched but she continued on, "it all means, perhaps, that you are one of the Godspeakers," that was definitely farfetched but she had faith enough in the gods to know such things were possible.

Mia started off-subject slightly, "They're always blurred, everything is blurred, even the voice ... like a strange nightmare that I can't, can't—"

"Understand," Niemhe gave her suggestion.

"Yes!" Mia accepted the word.

"Well, Mia, the next time you have a dream, you can tell me all about it and I will believe you, ok."

Mia nodded her head and beamed a little, then left the room.

Niemhe then wondered about the dream she had had the previous night.

The dream she had had whilst her boy was taken.

CHAPTER 27
IN A DAY

Elisia had arrived at her destination; she removed the wrappings and the mask that had hugged her face tightly, across her desert journey.

She stared upon her destination, the southern, sandstone city, Sairoh: home to fine swordsmen, grand architecture and Askarian historic knowledge, enough to rival that of the elves.

The note had arrived by courier to Elisia two days after her husband and his companions had left to the elven city, she still had the note in her knapsack:

Dear Countess Elisia of Clan Clairn,

It has come to my attention that you are in possession of an adventurous spirit and with no manner of other peoples willing to engage in this task and with most other adventurers turning to ridiculously expensive hired thugs, if you would accept my offer, as a friend and ally, I would task you this quest and offer you reward for your work. I understand at this time of year, a journey down south through the Arizail Desert is not the easiest nor most relaxing or desirable venture ever so if you reject my offer, I understand why.

A swift reply would be excellent.

Regards,

Althalos Timed-Tail, Lord of Sairoh, Head of Clan Gordanyes, Representative of Elibra for the Council of Askaria

Elisia had heard of Althalos, that he was an amazing fighter with any weapon, trained as a child in his jungle homeland of Mirrorlare under his elf race, the Dökkálfar, who had taught him with strict fighting regimes.

Word was that he had become even stronger since the death of his wife, Aledril, killed by marauders outside the city (Elisia expected Althalos's enlarged strength came from a thirst for vengeance).

Elisia remembered that Althalos did not join the other lords at the Snow-Born Council meeting, that he had had his hands full with something so important that he had decided not to attend the discussion regarding the Malice of Snow.

Elisia wondered if whatever had kept Althalos from the meeting, would be the thing she had been called to help with...

Elisia looked upon the gates, they glimmered in the face of the sun and it was hard to make out that they were made of pure gold.

Elisia went up to the guards who were clad in bronze armour and wore masked helmets, crested with orange feathers.

"What are your intentions upon entrance into great city Sairoh," one of them asked in a deep, manly voice.

"You'll find my intentions lie in a conversation with your lord," Elisia revealed the letter as proof.

The guard scanned the letter carefully before giving a hand signal to another guard who walked off in the direction of a lever, the soldier inserted a key into the lever before pulling it.

"Glad to see someone finally accepting Lord Althalos's 'quest'," the soldier exclaimed.

Elisia didn't like the emphasis the soldier had put on the word 'quest'.

The gate slowly opened behind them.

The soldier drummed his fingers on his leg whilst waiting.

Soon enough, the gate was open.

Elisia made for the entrance and as she did, the guard called after her.

"Good luck on your quest, Countess Elisia."

The guards all laughed.

The gate closed slowly behind Elisia as she walked forward into the city.

Inside, Elisia was greeted with the hustle and bustle of the market and the pure feeling of intimidation before the Palace of 40,000 Deaths.

The legend behind the palace was that centuries ago, the palace was created by 50, 000 slaves, the palace was meant to be sky-high but as it entered later stages, the not completely set material of the lower tower collapsed underneath the weight of the above, the higher tower collapsed killing the estimated amount of 40, 000 slaves by either crushing them or catching them in the setting sandstone cement to become part of the tower, suffocated, killed and confined.

The last remaining 10,000 slaves were hoisted onto giant spears and impaled slowly, as punishment for their failure in building the palace.

Elisia saw some soldiers heading towards her, who then escorted her through the palace.

The corridors she was transported through were dimly lit by braziers and the walls were almost completely decorated by preserved faces which bore looks of agony and distress paralysed there, the only part of the walls that weren't faceless, was where orange banners adorned with black scorpions, hung, the banners of Clan Gordanyes.

"Just through here, madam Elisia," one of her escort guards showed her through a pair of heavy doors, into a large room with an even larger balcony.

The room held a double bed, an office area and one huge table with golden animal heads engraved into it.

"Ah, Elisia, in all honesty, I wasn't expecting you, you didn't reply to my letter," Althalos stood up from behind his table, he was a dark shade of grey in skin colour due to his race.

"No, I thought that in the time it would take for the courier to do the journey again, I could have delivered the letter myself."

"Proving your intelligence right away, Elisia, I believe I have chosen the right person for the job already."

"Yes, and what exactly is this job," Elisia inquired.

"Well, you see I may have lied slightly to get you here."

"About what."

"The men, I've hired sixteen different men for this job so far ... not one has come back," Althalos diverted his eyes for a moment.

"How come?"

"I am not sure," Althalos replied, "that is why I need you."

"Well, where am I headed?"

"There are some ruins outside the city, we had begun excavation there to see what the ruins would yield us, unfortunately, our investor recently backed out from this operation and so I decided to go out on my own to the ruins, to find out why..." Althalos walked out onto the balcony, "it was horrible, all the miners there, fifty-three in total, dead, like they had had their faces cut off, I quickly escaped the site, I had never encountered a force capable of killing that many men."

"And so, you want me, a lesser fighter than you, I'm sure, to go out into this death trap."

"Yes, and the reason I have asked you of this is that although you may not be as skilled in combat as I, I have no doubt your intelligence, in such situation, exceeds mine."

Elisia nodded her head, "Don't expect much more knowledge into all of this than you already have, I can't see myself getting too close to the site after what you've told me, you'll just have to hope that my reckless spirit is intact today."

"I am aware of the amount of return I will get from this investigation and at this point, any bit of information would be good, and you will be rewarded no matter what you find, if anything at all."

"Well, in that case, I'll accept this quest," Elisia hoped she hadn't just sealed her fate.

Elisia then understood why the guards were finding this 'quest' so funny: it was because it wasn't a quest at all, it was a death trap.

"We rest here," Borgian talked to his horse and patted it on the side of the neck, he jumped off.

He had been riding the whole day so far and felt that both he and his horse needed some rest.

They had stopped at a clearing under a large oak, he took a glance at what lay ahead of him next on his journey, Nevara's Pass, the snowy northern mountain range that the Tower of Night inhabited.

Borgian looked up to the top of the mountains but his vision of the mountain's peaks was obscured by low clouds.

He groaned.

He looked at the map he had pocketed from Hymir's altar room to clarify which one of the peaks held the tower, unfortunately, it seemed to be the highest one.

Borgian felt the cold winds strike his face as he set up his bed for the night, he untied his travel sack from his horse's saddle and revealed two blankets Mazdol had lent him from the longhouse, the blankets were made of premium materials and lined, internally, with tiger skins.

Borgian tried to imagine what the famous tigers of Crowned Isle looked like, he had heard they bore golden fur, red eyes and teeth like the weapons of the tribes that had almost driven them to extinction.

Borgian set up the blankets underneath the large oak and added his cloak to it, he fell onto it and moved into the warmth.

He entered a deep sleep.

"So, make this clear for me, would you, I have to kill her, and that is all?" Mazdol asked finally.

"Yes, sir, and it must be you specifically, Zensi is the only thing altering the crown's allegiance towards you, with her out the way, and no less, by your hand, the crown will be yours," the historian relayed.

"If only she wasn't so stubborn ... I take her and everything from her, and yet she struggles out of my grasp, and now, she's gone straight into hiding..." Borgian then remembered something, "she was at the battle, she was the woman," Mazdol thought for a second before looking to a soldier guarding the door, "bring me Bogstot, he'll reveal the truth—or he will die."

"Has the queen come to a conclude," Chief Veirimen of Harphia inquired.

"Yes, madam Zensi has declared for the body of the stewardess, Georlia Nighren, to be retrieved and given her funeral rites and for the villagers of Harphia to be taught how to defend themselves, we will offer those who wish to fight, to Borgian Steel when the time comes," Aelius told, "these are the demands of our queen, and after the Malice of Snow has been defeated, we shall progress to urge the city leaders to join the fight against Mazdol and reclaim the city of Mezal, that lies above."

"Good, let these demands be written on paper, for history to remember, they shall be put into motion straight away, this meeting is closed."

The inner-circle fled from the room, bowing to Zensi and Frienz as they went.

Zensi spotted Arntia talking to her father, "So it has truly begun," she exclaimed excitedly.

"Yes daughter, it has been decided, the fate of the Aloks, the fate of Harphia and the fate of Askaria."

Ariesa Herginn sat, dismally, on the throne of Talgrin city, she was ruling temporarily by the side of her brother whilst her father, Mazdol, took control of Mezal city.

She had been released from the prison she had been held captive in during her father's liberation of Mezal, only a few days after the event and yet that was enough to change her, the truth had sunk in.

Ariesa's world had become a chaotic one over the past few months and weeks; She had come to the realisation that to her father, she was just a tool, she had been left in control of a city ridden with brothels, black markets and death, and she had lost Frienz to this feud.

She didn't know what was scarier, the fact that after everything, she still loved him or the fact that she had the feeling, he still loved her.

What she was doing on the throne now, was addressing the problems of citizens, she was handling it in the opposite way her father would.

An elderly woman approached now, "Please, dear, I have little food to feed my children and their children, and not enough money to pay rent, please help me."

Arntia looked at the poor woman, "Give this woman enough Heads for 3 years of rent and food."

"What?! That's about 1000 Heads!" a man of the Talgrin council exclaimed.

"Yes, I'm aware of that, see to it she gets that exact amount of money," Arntia glared at the man.

The elderly woman's eyes brimmed with tears, "Thank you so much, kind dear, I will not forget this, thank you again."

"Arntia, please reconsider," the councilman asked of her.

Arntia smiled and said simply, "No, this woman *will* receive 1000 Heads, I am not my father."

What she did then was definitely the opposite of what her father would do.

She looked at her brother, he nodded at her.

She knew she'd still have to marry him someday; she might as well start getting used to him, now.

"Mia, don't you see, you belong to this world, it owns you and you own it, don't worry about the other world, let go of your worries, don't worry," the voice spoke.

"But I want to worry, I want to help," Mia spoke.

"Oh, petty child, go worry, we will speak again soon, I enjoy watching you and to see how your world changes after every dream we share, as the children continue to aid me."

CHAPTER 28
TWO BROTHERS

The sun was rising, as were the Sundered Isles on the horizon.

Aron watched as Amateir City came into sight, home to his family, Clan Amateir, the clan to which the city was named after.

The ship that Aron travelled on, the Black Basilisk, docked at the city's port.

As Aron dismounted the ship, he was greeted by a couple of his family's soldiers, "Good to see you, Lord Aron, your parents wish to see you."

"Of course," Aron replied, "but first, I must pay this gentleman who offered to take me across the Faithful Bay."

Aron turned to the captain and paid him a sum, much heftier than that of which he should have paid.

The captain gave a fruity smile, "Thank you, I'll be able to buy food for a year with this."

The captain shook hands with Aron and was off back to Askaria.

Aron followed the soldiers through the city, taking his time to admire the smell of cooked fish lingering on the salty air, the markets selling the strangest assortments of delicious food, curious artefacts and on the rare occasion, for the children, the best toffee sweets around.

The people of Amateir were never in a rush, always equipped with their manners, and wearing vibrant colours; purples, greens and blues.

Amateir City homed the most respectful, knowledgeable and empathic of people who always tried to solve problems with peace, when they could at least, due to the quantity of problems caused by Clan Amateir holding secrets, frequently causing violence.

Atop the hill could Clan Amateir's large, sea-overlooking villa be seen.

Originally, the villa was created as a cathedral to honour the Edicryte god, Alekj, king of the sea, and represented by a blue squid.

Aron was led into the villa by the soldiers who then resumed their posts, protecting the building.

He walked over to the balcony and greeted his father and mother.

His father, Oprus, wore teal robes and had a layer of white stubble decorating his chin, his eyes were blue like the sea.

His mother, Valhea, however, had green eyes and long, flowing white hair down to her hips.

"And my youngest son finally returns," Oprus exclaimed.

"Father, mother, it is good to see you again."

"Aron, we need to discuss something ... important with you," Valhea informed him.

"What is it?" Aron questioned, slightly worried.

"It's the council, they want you to take over my place when I die," Oprus told.

"But I'm not the eldest."

"No, you are not, but the Tournament of Alekj is coming up and they want you and your eldest brother, Tremis, to be the main attraction, they want you to fight to the death, you have three days to prepare."

"But father—"

"I'm sorry, this is out of our hands, Councillor Yokvon has the whole council, plus the people, behind him, the punishment for not taking part is execution."

Aron fled the house, and soon enough, found himself sitting in the Buried Treasure Pub, thinking, he paid the barkeeper for a Honeywhip Brewery Ale.

The ale was cold but had a subtle warmth to it.

Aron began to wonder what would happen to him if he couldn't defeat his brother; he'd have to kill him, or he would die.

At that moment, he was interrupted in his thoughts, by a man sitting down next to him.

Aron looked to see who it was: It was his second oldest brother, Rambol, the member of the Amateir family disgraced and despised by the people for his debaucherous ways and tendency to spend Amateir's money on betting in different lands.

Rambol was obviously drunk at the current moment, he looked at Aron with one eye open and talked with a slur, "I know people … who'll make yeh life hard."

Aron tried to ignore his meaningless mumbling but found it to be an extremely difficult task.

He ended up leaving the pub and went back to the house.

If he was going to practise for the fight, he knew exactly who to do it with.

His third oldest brother, an expert fighter and general of Amateir's troops, he was a mute but that did not change the fact he was a fearsome combatant.

"Miscen," that was his brother's name, the one he addressed him by when he saw him in the courtyard, "I have three days to practise, and I'm not going to lose this fight, I need your help, teach me how to fight like a warrior of the Sundered Isles."

"My daughter is gone!" chanted a woman, "my daughter is gone!"

Niemhe came out of her hut to see what the noise that had awakened her, was about.

A crowd of villagers flocked around the woman who had been shouting, whispering such things as: "Our village is truly cursed," and 'We are all doomed, when the children run out, we'll be next."

That day, a wealthy family from the village left with their child, other parents begged them to take theirs too.

No such kindness was granted.

The family that left that day, were the only family wealthy enough to afford transport outside of the village.

Niemhe took it upon herself to check the missing girl's house, she wanted to help and let the other families know that she shared their pain.

Inside the house, Niemhe found nothing until she entered the girl's room, what she found was a staff, sticky—with drying blood.

Niemhe had to fight back tears, she wondered where her own son was, and then she thought, Mia, the staff, maybe she had seen it in a dream.

Niemhe needed to know, she walked outside to find Mia already waiting.

"He talked to me last night, you know, he told me not to worry about this world, he said I control the world of dreams, but I need to go back, see it all again," Mia came out with suddenly.

"Mia, did you see a staff in your dreams?" Niemhe placed her hands on the girl's shoulders, forcing her to concentrate.

"Yes, the Staff of Souls, it communicates with the children," Mia replied calmly.

"What? What do you mean?"

"I've ... I've got to go," Mia announced before running off, too fast for Niemhe to catch up with.

Niemhe sighed, she felt helpless.

CHAPTER 29
DEATH BEGINS TO BREED

The frigid snow blasted Borgian's weather-beaten face, he adjusted his hood, trying to make it so he could feel the warmth of the fur insulation.

He needed to stop but he couldn't, he had a quest to complete, a sword to reclaim.

He continued up the mountain and eventually, came across two paths, one led straight forward, the other lay on an incline, going up.

Borgian knew he had to go up, he wished he could choose the forward path, but he couldn't.

He went higher and eventually, his body temperature began to kick in, he felt warmer, and he smiled for a moment.

And then, there was a movement of snow beneath his feet.

Borgian froze in fear for a moment, and then the ground collapsed beneath him, his footing was lost but he quickly extended a hand in just enough time to save him from falling to his death.

He didn't dare look down.

If his hand slipped, now, he would surely die.

Borgian, with his other hand, now tested a gap in the ice, to check it was safe.

He believed that he could hoist himself up, using it as a boost.

What he hoped would happen, did not, the ice caved in on his hand when he tried to grip the ledge.

Borgian hissed in pain.

Borgian would have to remove his glove to stop the ice from crushing the bones in his fingers.

He managed to slip the glove off and then boost himself up on the ice, back onto the path.

The cold instantly gripped his hand.

"Ah, Bogstot," Mazdol spoke slyly, "you came."

"Mazdol, 'ow can I 'elp?" Bogstot questioned, wary of Mazdol's slyness.

"I would like to ask you to go back to the day the Malice of Snow came to Mezal, and find something for me, you see, on the day the Disavowed attacked, you rode into the city, accompanied by two strangers, one, a women, I don't have women in my army, Bogstot, so if you could explain who she was for me."

Bogstot stayed silent as Mazdol waited for an answer.

"We should walk, perhaps a stride will relieve your memory."

Zensi heard footsteps, she urged the Seekers to hurry up, they were trying to carry Georlia's body but were currently failing and then, when Mazdol came around the corner, retreated to the shadows, with Georlia.

"They just needed some motivation," Zensi thought.

Zensi could hear Mazdol was with another, Bogstot.

"She was a common woman an' a peasant, we couldn't just leave her to die there on the road," Bogstot argued.

"You lie, Bogstot," Mazdol exposed Bogstot, "I am your superior, you may be a lord, but you are just like the others, you're a lapdog looking for some recognition, and you do so by forcing yourself into the pocket of a pretender, Zensi."

Zensi flinched in the darkness.

Bogstot suddenly went red, and in the blink of an eye, weapons were drawn, they began to circle.

"I heard about what yeh said ter me wife, everyone knows, yeh declared war," Bogstot clashed blades with Mazdol.

They were fighting ferociously now, the two were utterly distracted, Zensi signalled for the Seekers to carry the body away, Zensi took one last glance back at the battle, and then she was gone.

She wished she had more loyal fighters like Bogstot.

From out of nowhere, Mazdol swung his axe up, catching Bogstot off guard, and cutting into Bogstot's stomach.

"Who was that woman!?" Mazdol shouted out again, "tell me or I'm going to leave you to your fate."

"Fuck off Herginn, long live Clan Alok."

With those final words, in anger and frustration, Mazdol delivered the final blow, with his axe, carving into the crouched Bogstot's soldiers, and not stopping.

Blood sprayed Mazdol, over and over again, until he was painted red, and Bogstot's upper body had been completely minced.

"Finally, I wondered when you'd shut up."

"Night's drawing on, Mia," Niemhe announced, "you should get home."

Mia had been telling Niemhe about the dream she had been elusive about before.

Mia nodded, "Back to my realm."

Niemhe watched Mia walk out the door, something dark was haunting that girl.

Elisia walked out from the city of Sairoh, she could already see the rumoured fires in the distance and there the strange, alien chanting.

Elisia mounted a steed and rode off in the direction of the fire and its accompanying pillar of smoke.

She rode west.

The job she was carrying out was not something she particularly wanted to do at night, but, apparently, it was the only time it happened at.

When she drew near to the source of these strange events, she dismounted her horse and proceeded with caution.

Before her, was a giant mount of soil with a few ruined stone structures embedded in it, the fire seemed to be coming from the stone floor in front of the mound of dirt—it held a pattern of illuminated oil.

The pattern was of a four-fingered claw.

She then noticed the people standing around it, the people chanting, they wore black, chainmail decorated robes and masks showing sad faces.

She had heard mention of this ritual in a book before, but she couldn't remember which one.

She had information to bring back to Sairoh and as she turned back towards the city, she heard the cultists begin to speak normally.

"How long now? Must we pray every day?"

"We pray until the daughter of dragons arrives from the island with the foreign king."

"And how long will that be?"

"After the snow ceases and the path is set, then the purging begins."

Elisia had heard enough now.

"Thank you, I'll have that information sourced back to my libraries, perhaps, if you are curious, you could do the same too, a little annoying how these people didn't reveal any more information about who they were, but, never the less, you have helped my city, here are your rewards."

Althalos passed Elisia a collection of four books; Woe of the White Elves, Curse of Sycron, Chronicles of the Malice of Snow, Symbols of Ice.

"I hope you find these books aid you in your quest against the Malice of Snow, some of the only books on the subject away from the southern lands," Althalos verbalized.

"Thank you, I'm sure they will be of use," Elisia exclaimed, "now, I must get over to Mezal to collect my husband, best go before the sandstorm strikes."

Aron saw the sun beginning to fall under the horizon, "Should we stop, brother?"

Miscen, Aron's mute brother and general of Amateir's guard, revealed his wax tablet and began to write.

Miscen became a mute after his tongue was cut out by a pirate king, since then, he had resorted to his tablet which now read: 'a warrior will fight through night and day, we will begin, practising now, with real weapons.'

Miscen nodded at Aron to signify his choice being right before picking up his choice weapon, a sabre blade, made from a silver-coated tiger's tooth.

What caught Aron's eye along the weapon rack, was a double-edged halberd, he picked it up, it was surprisingly light.

As the two began their battle, they only fought for five seconds before they heard a shrill scream from within the villa.

The two brothers faced each other, worried, before entering the villa.

They ascended the stairs, upwards, into the sleeping quarters where Oprus, Aron and Miscen's father, lay, bleeding out on the bed, a hole through his chest spurting out blood.

Valhea, the two's mother, lay with him on the bed, cradling Oprus' corpse.

Miscen was in shock, paralysed in position, whilst Aron went over to his mother, trying to comfort her and find out what happened.

He found out nothing.

"Who could have done this?!" Valhea shouted out in anguish.

"I ... I have an idea who, but you wouldn't believe me if I told you."

The moon was up.

7 days remained.

CHAPTER 30
SANTERUIS AMATEIR DARVOR

Aron sat down, he was waiting, he wore grey robes as the rest of the city would be, today.

In Amateir, grey was the colour of mourning.

Aron's father, Oprus Amateir, was to be buried under the New Cathedral of Alejk, the second cathedral of Alejk built due to the fact the first one was home to Clan Amateir.

The funeral would be the last event in which Tremis and Aron could meet peacefully, before the battle.

When the time came, Aron proceeded to the funeral where Oprus would be flayed before his burial and have his skin thrown into the sea so that as their tradition decreed, the person could return to their two original sources, the sea and the earth.

After the procession which Aron noticed Tremis was absent at, Aron returned home and sat down with Miscen to enjoy a glass of Black Blossom Wine.

Aron toasted, "To our father, a great man, a great leader, a husband and a father, rest his soul."

The two clinked their glasses and tipped the sweet nectar down their throats.

Then came the voice, "Could Lord Aron come forth to the House of Battle, due to Tremis being next in line to the throne until this battle begins and finishes, his decree must be acknowledged that the Battle of Alejk shall be held today!" The town crier concluded.

Miscen exchanged a worried look with Aron.

"Bring me my halberd, let's get this over with, once and for all," Aron commanded, "I will avenge our father."

Miscen pulled a puzzled face in response to Aron's last statement.

Aron knew something Miscen didn't, that Tremis had killed their father.

Aron was ready, Miscen had gifted him his armour, bought by the socialites of the city, and had sharpened his halberd for him.

He gave it a few swings before the councillor announced the start of the battle, "People of Amateir, today is a day of change for our city, today two brothers fight for the throne of Amateir, one brother with a right to ascend and one with the favouring of the public who wished for this battle to take place, now, without further ado, Santeruis Amateir Darvor."

The battle gates opened, and the fight began, Aron went for the first blow but was easily blocked by Tremis and his kukri.

"Come on, Aron, I thought you would have learnt a thing or two, being at the wretched land of war for so long," Tremis mocked.

Aron clenched his jaw in annoyance, almost forgetting to deflect a quick blow from Tremis' kukri.

"Give up brother," Tremis tried again, this time attacking Aron's hand, the kukri caught and Tremis let go, leaving Aron to remove it.

When Aron did pull it from his hand, he aimed for Tremis' shoulder, it went exactly where Aron wanted it to go, straight through Tremis' shoulder blade.

Tremis was vulnerable and as he reached for another dagger, Aron swept his halberd under Tremis' legs, knocking him down.

Tremis fell to the ground and then whilst he thought Aron was unsuspecting, tried to plunge his newly unsheathed dagger into Aron's stomach.

Aron quickly jumped back, however, avoiding Tremis' dagger and then slamming his halberd down into Tremis' weapon arm.

Tremis was defeated, he was at Aron's mercy.

"Now, listen brother, I know what you've done so admit it to me, admit you killed our father, and I might spare you," Aron whispered in Tremis' ear.

"You weren't meant to kill me, you fool," Tremis laughed, "I misguided our parents for this purpose, and it wasn't me who killed our parents, it was Yokvon, all I ever wanted was a free pass out of this world in the glory of battle, now, you'll be hunted," Tremis revealed his bloody teeth in a wide grin, "you're...the... killer."

Tremis gave a short laugh and then fell back, dead, in his own puddle of blood.

The crowd looked horrified, what Tremis had said was true, Aron wasn't meant to kill him, he was just meant to bring him to the floor.

Aron took sight of Councillor Yokvon, he looked scarily happy.

Yokvon was responsible for everything.

"Murder! Murder! He has killed his own brother, power has consumed him, arrest him!" Yokvon shouted out at once.

Many of the soldiers seemed to follow Yokvon's orders however those that had honour and remembered they were paid off the Amateir family's payroll, stayed true.

"Lord Aron, we are at your command, what do we do?"

"We fight."

"You know where you must go, don't you, Mia."

"Yes, I've seen it before, through your eyes," Mia told the voice.

"Find it for me, and I will return the missing children."

"You were born there, weren't you?" Mia inquired.

"Indeed child, and I can be reborn there," the voice told.

"I can find it if you promise you'll stop what's going on," Mia stated.

"I promise."

"Then, we have a deal."

Borgian had lit a fire, he was roasting wolves on it, that he'd hunted on his journey up the mountain.

He took a bite of the wolf to then spit it straight out, it was still raw.

A searing pain in Borgian's left hand then reminded him of the situation, Borgian looked down at his hand, it had turned black and a numbness seemed to be coming over it and his wrist.

Borgian tried to move his fingers but he couldn't.

He hadn't thought about what taking the glove off, might have caused to happen to his hand.

Borgian could only see one way, at this point, from stopping the problem getting worse.

He revealed a knife, he never thought he'd end up using it on himself and heated it above the fire until it became red hot.

He steadied his arm on a log he had cut for the fire and with a shaking hand, brought the knife up and with hesitation, closed his eyes and brought the knife down.

He screamed in pain, it was unbearable, his dead hand rolled off the log and coloured the snow red.

Next, Borgian took out his sword and heated it above the fire, it was better for this job because it was wider, and then, then nothing, Borgian couldn't subject himself to any more pain but he

189

had to do this, there was blood spraying everywhere and Borgian was fading in and out of consciousness.

He needed to do this.

He needed to do this.

And then, Borgian brought the flat of his blade to the stump at the end of his arm.

He held it there for as long as he could before shoving his arm's stump into the snow and throwing his sword to the floor.

The stump was wrapped in linen after that.

The pain had eased slightly about half an hour later, and then, the hunger kicked in.

Borgian went to check on the wolf again, he didn't dare touch it, from under the animal's skin, many maggots were now crawling.

Borgian's discarded hand was beginning to look tastier and tastier and eventually, the wolf was thrown off the fire and the hand was skewered.

Mia felt the night's cold embrace, it was time she headed for the gate, remembering a path she had seen through the eyes of the spirit.

Mia knew the spirit was a malevolent one and would possibly devour her soul or something along those lines if given the chance.

Maybe that was what the evil deity intended to do when Mia got to its birthplace.

But Mia didn't care at this point, no matter the cost, she needed to put the village before herself.

Before the gates, however, she noticed Niemhe standing before her, "What are you doing out so late?" She asked.

Mia stayed silent.

"What am I kidding, I know why you're out here, I hear it too you know, I heard the spirit before my boy was stolen."

"So, you're not going to stop me," Mia accented.

"No, Mia, how could I, I can't resist the call, I shouldn't expect you to be able to, we are not descendants of Kinsia, we are descendants of Krysos, the Dycrite god of omens and illusions, we are the offspring of evil," Niemhe opened the gate, "the quicker we leave Stone Mount, the safer everyone here will be, we must get my son back, we must awaken Krysos in his mortal form," Niemhe finished.

Mia nodded and the two strode off, down the path, south, away from Stone Mount...

CHAPTER 31
SET IN MOTION

"Open the gates, madam Elisia returns!"

The gates opened, and the guards bowed before her.

This surprised her after her last confrontation with Mazdol.

"Where is Lord Mazdol? I have a delivery for him," Elisia asked.

"He was last seen in the library, my lady."

"And, my husband?" she inquired.

"Sorry, my lady, I haven't seen him."

Elisia headed into Mezal city and turned a right corner, the library stood in front of her.

Inside the library, Mazdol could be seen reading a bulky, rough, untitled book intently.

Elisia walked over to him.

"Mazdol."

"Elisia, collecting your husband, I suppose."

"Do you see any other reason for me being here after our last conversation," Elisia stated rudely.

"No, I don't."

"Well, actually there is," Elisia told him.

She passed him the stack of books Althalos had rewarded her with, to Mazdol.

"Why?" He questioned her.

"Because we're not enemies until the Malice of Snow is defeated, now, have you seen my husband?"

"No, I haven't," Mazdol lied.

Elisia gave him a suspicious look, she noticed how his voice changed when he answered her.

Mazdol went to take the books but Elisia suddenly took them back.

"A change of heart, hmm," Mazdol gave her a look.

She nodded her head, "Yes," she said plainly.

Mazdol departed from the library, raising Elisia's suspicions even higher.

Suddenly, from behind Elisia, a bookshelf moved aside and Zensi Alok stepped out from the darkness.

"Hello, Elisia."

Elisia stared at Zensi for a while before talking, "Hello, Zensi, glad to see you are well but..."

"There are passageways under the city that even I didn't know about before, they link up to almost everywhere in Mezal," Zensi explained, "I need to discuss something important with you."

Zensi disappeared back into the shadows, and Elisia, intrigued, followed.

The bookshelf slotted back into position, behind her.

The tunnel was lit up by the torch Zensi held in her hand.

They were in silence until they reached the passageway to Harphia and until the passageway was open.

"This is Harphia."

Zensi walked Elisia through the village until they stopped at the gate of a large garden speckled with gravestones.

"What's going on, Zensi? I need to know," Elisia urged her, impatiently, and with worry.

"You will see," Zensi responded solemnly, "I will warn you that it's not the nicest sight, but we tried to make him look as ready for the gods as possible."

Elisia became significantly more worried after Zensi said this.

The two women entered the garden of graves and ascended a slight incline that took them to where two bodies were laid down on an altar, a grave had been dug on either side of the stone slab.

One among them, Elisia recognised as Georlia, the other one, Elisia recognised as Bogstot, despite the fact that only his lower body remained, and his upper body had been replaced with the top half of a mannequin, his face painted on and his emblem on his chest.

Then the realisation kicked in, her husband was dead.

"Gods, please, no..." Elisia whispered under her breath, tears began to gather in her eyes before streaming down her face, "who did this?" She asked Zensi.

"Your husband fought well against him, he was loyal to me and to you, and understood that there's another war going on, beyond the one for the crown," Zensi bowed her head.

"But who killed him!?" Elisia asked as her sadness started to amount to anger.

"We managed to reclaim what was left of his body ... after Mazdol killed him."

"What!?" Elisia shouted out in a strangled voice consisting of fury and anguish.

That night, Zensi and Elisia comforted each other as they watched two of their friends disappear out of their world forever.

The bodies were gently dropped into their graves, their rites were given, and their names engraved on the altar separating the burial places.

"We will get revenge," Zensi proclaimed, her eyes still fixed on Georlia's grave as the Seekers began shovelling dirt into it.

"I know," Elisia confirmed, "when the Battle of Winter finishes, if I'm still alive, I will march my men to Talgrin, and take it and his children from beneath him," Elisia stopped and looked at Zensi, "come back to my city with your Seekers and join me, the city of Drumdallg stands with you, Queen Zensi."

"Of course, and the War of the Crown truly begins," Zensi announced.

"Yes, and we will win."

"Go, go!" Aron shouted, "defend the east side, we need an advantage!"

Aron Amateir watched as the forces of Amateir City marched against each other.

It was the council against the clan.

The city had collapsed in on itself.

It was madness.

Miscen was by Aron's side, giving out orders, using hand signals.

They fought against Grand Councillor Yokvon who had set Aron up, made him look like a power consumed tyrant and turned the city's people against him.

Crowds ran out the way of the battle in terror.

"There's no longer hope for your clan, Aron, the dictatorship of Amateir shall become a democracy," Yokvon declared, "give up your fight."

"What do you hope to gain from this, Yokvon!"

"Respect, protection, power, things that all men desire," Yokvon announced.

A ball of flame catapulted overhead.

"The tools of a coward, Yokvon, of course, a man so weak would desire those things," Aron watched as Yokvon was suddenly backed up with a horde of soldiers.

Yokvon went red, "I will not be humiliated, I am high councillor of Amateir and I will soon be ruler of this city, kill him."

"Yokvon, don't do this!" Aron shouted out as he defended himself against the oncoming threat, "don't you think there's been enough bloodshed today."

Yokvon smiled, showing the most prominent wrinkles of his face, "Come now, Aron, I better not have killed your father for nothing."

At the mention of his father, Aron threw the sword, he was using, to the ground, and revealed his halberd from the scabbard on his back.

Miscen's soldiers advanced on Yokvon's.

Miscen raised his hand and then closed it, signalling his soldiers to attack.

Blood sprayed steel and the battle was set in motion.

CHAPTER 32
THE TOWER

Borgian Steel had caught sight of it, the Tower of Night standing tall atop the peak.

It was an eerie sight, the dark edifice in the snow.

Borgian was exhausted, hungry, pale with cold, he didn't know if he could face what was inside in his current state, even if he was only against a blacksmith.

Borgian progressed forward, he could see the snow, heavy, on the breeze, the darkening clouds, the peaks circling the area, and as Borgian pressed on, the tower seemed to look taller and the windows seemed to darken.

Borgian rested his hand on the pommel of his blade, he was ready.

"Borgian Steel, I knew you would come, to reclaim the Ethril Blade," a voice rang out, Borgian noted that it sounded different from Rolgirtis.

"Do not hinder me, evil spirit!" Borgian yelled out.

"Hinder you? But of course not, I understand you aim to kill the Blue Knight, Rolgirtis, one of my enemies, I have wanted him dead for years, and after he forged the Sword of Fading, he consumed my power, found out how to make himself immortal and took control of my curse."

Borgian realised who the voice belonged to, it was the malevolent Dycrite of death, war and pestilence: Sycron, the creator of the Malice of Snow.

"My worshipper thought bringing the blade to my shrine would please me, but I would rather have the retched blade in the hands of you."

"Why?" Borgian wondered.

"Because I am not a mortal and cannot touch the Ethril Blade and defeat Rolgirtis myself as you can. When Rolgirtis dies, my power will return, and the curse will fall back into my domain, my worshipper has been punished for his insolence, you will find him easy to defeat in his state, don't fail me."

Borgian was, once again, left alone in the cold.

He placed his hand on the door of the tower but didn't need to pull.

The door suddenly burst open and broke, off its hinges, the door smashed into Borgian, knocking him far backwards, towards the edge of the mountain.

Borgian only had a few seconds to rebalance himself and get up.

He faced Hymir, his eyes were gone and only red, burnt sockets remained, his arms were stretched thin and dragged on the floor.

It was horrible, Hymir was a monstrosity.

"Hymir, just give me the blade."

Hymir turned to where Borgian's voice had boomed from.

"No, Borgian, our fates are intertwined and already sealed."

Borgian went to ready his blade but it was stuck, frozen in its scabbard.

When Borgian looked up again, Hymir was there, he pounced on Borgian and both of them fell off the side of the mountain.

Hymir kicked Borgian in the shins whilst they turned around in the air.

Borgian tried his hardest to be on top so to soften the fall.

When Borgian did get on top of Hymir, he intended for it to stay that way, he delivered painful blows to Hymir's face, and as they reached the ground, Borgian stopped punching Hymir and readied himself.

'THUMP,' they crashed into the ground.

Hymir was still alive due to the thickness of the snow, but not for long.

Hymir's legs were broken and Borgian took the chance to reclaim the Ethril Blade from Hymir's belt and to stab it into his chest.

Hymir's corpse froze, a layer of frost spread from his wound and encapsulated his body.

Hymir's blood stained the snow.

Borgian stood up, victorious, but only to fall back down.

His vision went blurry and he fell into a deep sleep.

As did the rest of Askaria...

CHAPTER 33
BATTLE OF WINTER

Borgian woke up, the building he awoke in was shadowed and dingy but still recognisable as the dungeon below Mezal's palace.

Borgian wondered what had happened, how in hell had he got here.

Around him were many other people starting to wake up too; citizens, lords, soldiers.

He spotted Mazdol from across the room.

"Borgian, is that you?" Mazdol wondered aloud.

"Yes, I think," Borgian's mind was very fuzzy, "what happened?"

"What happened was an effect of the curse," an elv of the Ljósálfar race explained, "the curse releases an effluvium that puts all people within its spread, who are not of elven race or below ground, to sleep, we have heard the miasma spread as far as the Crowned Citadel down to the Sundered Isles, all people have been herded to their cities of birth."

"Who are you?" Borgian asked.

"I am Ivoia the third, nineteenth steward of Raschel Oki Frindal, City of Prosper," Ivoia announced.

"How long have we been asleep for?" Mazdol inquired.

"Long enough for us to find Elisia Clairn and Zensi Alok in the sewers of Mezal, and long enough for them to take over Talgrin city, I was surprised they didn't reclaim Mezal instead, in all honesty, but humans do have different minds from us elves … one day remains," Ivoia stated calmly.

"What?" Mazdol and Borgian chorused.

"Where are my children? How did this happen?" Mazdol bombarded Ivoia with questions.

"Your children were captured, a leverage of sort we believe they are being held as, and how it happened? Take a guess, all your soldiers were asleep, Mazdol."

"Wait, we only have one day left?" Borgian was worried.

"Yes, but there is good news, Elisia Clairn has managed to trace what material the Ethril Blade was made out of, using books she was rewarded with, by Althalos," Ivoia proclaimed, "my kind have already starting forging the required weapons out of the material, Tritahnium, made out of sapphires and silver and the snow itself, we will bring them to you before the battle begins, then we will depart."

"You're not fighting," Mazdol inquired inquisitively.

"No, we are elves of the Ljósálfar, we have a code to follow that protects us, one that says we must not fight wars that are not ours."

"But this is your war as well as ours, this is all of Askaria's battle to fight if we all hope to survive," Borgian explained.

"I am sorry, truly, but to disobey the code is to accept a death penalty."

"Can you at least rally the men?" Borgian questioned impatiently.

"No, because that job has been entrusted to you, Zensi wishes for you to retain a position as a primary leader in the battle, she trusts you very much."

Mazdol seemed annoyed at this proclamation, perhaps suspecting some sort of twisted betrayal was taking place.

"Do you know which cities are aiding us in this battle?"

"All but Hernight, apparently their problems with the Missionaries have escalated massively."

Borgian nodded, "To the Plains of the Patron then."

The people awoke in Amateir City.

Yokvon sat up and had little time to duck before Aron slammed his halberd down.

He had awoken before Yokvon.

"Get up!" Aron shouted.

Yokvon did, he raised his sword and they fought as everyone began to awaken around them, those that were still alive at least.

Aron watched Miscen whilst he fought, he was butchering many.

The blood began to spray and rain down upon the battle.

Soldiers began to switch sides and Yokvon began to lose those he fought were loyal to him.

"You can't buy loyalty, Yokvon, I thought you would have learnt that," Aron called out to Yokvon, trying to make himself heard over the sound of death.

Yokvon seemed to be quite skilled, Aron noticed, he decided he'd mock that somehow, Aron was trying to distract Yokvon by doing so, "It seems you've learnt some skills besides the ones you equip whilst in bed with the women you pay."

"Shut it, Aron, once you die, no one will ever face me again."

"Oh, but they will, they'll find out what you really are, and you will be repulsed and despised, I'm saving you from the pain you'll feel in later life."

Aron suddenly brought his halberd downwards and then right, hard, into Yokvon's leg.

"Surrender Yokvon and I'll grant you the mercy of a quick death."

Yokvon fell to the ground, not to surrender and beg for mercy, but due to how far Aron's halberd had cut into his leg.

"I'll never surrender to you, you disgusting mongrel," Yokvon spoke through gritted teeth.

"Fine, Miscen, escort Councillor Yokvon to the prisons and leave his wound to fester, do not treat it, everyone else, prepare yourselves, the Malice of Snow is upon Askaria, there's no saying it won't pass us."

"Yes, Lord Aron."

The battle ceased.

Ariesa Herginn and her brother, Stork, sat on a log.

Snow coated the ground and so Zensi had granted them the mercy of a dry place to sit.

The Plains of the Patron were populated with the soldiers of Mezal, Talgrin and Drumdallg, all under the command of Zensi Alok.

The only troops Mazdol had left now were those accompanying him at Mezal, and the infamous Army of Jerilla the bandit queen, that Mazdol had befriended.

The army could be seen over the horizon now.

Stork stared at his sister, making her feel uncomfortable, "You're beautiful, you know."

"Can you not!" Ariesa snapped back.

"Sorry sister, I'm just trying to fit into the relationship we'll have soon," Stork apologised.

"Don't be," Ariesa sighed, "I should probably start doing the same."

"It's not right, a sister should not marry her brother, she should have free will, she should be able to marry who she wants."

"There's no such thing as free will, brother, we are compelled to do as we are forced to, and even when we are not being forced to do something, we don't do it because we wrongly believe there is

203

something greater than us, we are controlled by others, and our fear of death, we focus on the immaterial to the point we don't live our lives just as our father does," Ariesa looked over the plains, she could see snow in the distance, "do you really believe, that in a world like this, that there are deities, freedom and an afterlife better than this one?"

Her brother said nothing.

"There isn't, if there were deities, we wouldn't be alive, the gods wouldn't have let a man like our father walk the earth, he would have never had us, we would never have had to experience the pains of life, heartbreak and deception."

Ariesa was filled with rage, as she sat on a log in the cold; her hands bound, captured by the enemy, in a star-crossed relationship with the enemy, soon to marry her brother against her will and in the crossfires of war.

"I wonder, if our mother was still alive, would she have been able to stop Mazdol from making the mistakes he has over the years," Frienz thought aloud.

"Maybe, or maybe not, from what I know, our mother belonged to another man, maybe she would have encouraged his mistakes, after all, she willingly slept with him, twice, despite the fact she was married."

"Maybe, we don't know enough about our mother," Frienz suggested.

"Maybe we need a conversation with our father, although perhaps not now, whilst a battle draws near, and we lie in the enemy's hands."

Zensi turned towards Ariesa and Stork now, she watched as they were taken away by her soldiers, back to Drumdallg.

She had decided against having them here, in case it set off Mazdol.

Perhaps, it wasn't the best time to anger him, when a battle that required his army, drew near.

Zensi watched the horizon as the Malice of Snow slowly crept forwards.

They all met in the heavy snow, all the armies of men and their commanding lords: Mazdol Herginn, Zensi Alok, Frienz Alok, Elisia Clairn, Arin Sheal, Althalos Gordanyes, Aminucilie Sahjan, Ulric Crewe, Terrowin Ceize and Borgian Steel.

"Are we all here, good," Zensi started but was interrupted.

"No, we are still missing Bogstot Clairn and Aramor Benortitien," Arin Sheal observed.

"Aramor will not be joining us due to problems with the Missionaries and Bogstot—"

"—Was butchered by Mazdol," Elisia finished her sentence, "hence why he no longer is in possession of his city or his children."

All the lords, including Borgian, shot Mazdol a look of disgust but no one dared say anything at this time.

The wind howled and the armies stood to attention, in waiting.

Hundreds of thousands of men in the cold.

The snow falling heavier and heavier, blinding everyone and freezing them in their armours.

Then Mazdol asked the question, "Shall we begin?"

Zensi announced, "Yes, we are assembled here, once more, as the Snow-Born Council to defeat the oncoming threat, a threat that we shall prevail against!"

The lords cheered.

"May the flames of our spirit melt the woe and terror of the snow," Mazdol continued.

"And the blood within our veins fuel our determination," Borgian sustained the battle cry.

"Together, we are strong, the clans and our peoples all united for one day, our victory is assured!" Zensi finished.

All the armies cheered and as they did, portals opened, and elves came rushing out of them, carrying large crates, there were about one thousand of them carrying about fifty weapons each.

When the crates were opened, the shimmering blue weapons could be seen within.

The armies equipped their weapons as they were passed around, the deadly tools of destruction, that were their only hope.

The sounds of metal and murmuring filled the air as all readied themselves.

The banners of each clan were held high.

Borgian thanked Ivoia as he passed by him, "Thank you, anything I can—"

"Borgian, don't go making promises you can't keep, you use to be a bandit, a disloyal, untrustworthy brand of person, and you have been in our prisons for two years before, this isn't for you or your people, this is for my kin, or at least you can try to believe that," Ivoia was gone, through one of the portals.

The portals closed to reveal the great masses of frigid snow and the unsettled winds that could be seen due to the white snowflakes it carried within.

It rolled across the plains, destroying and freezing anything in its path, hiding everything behind, with its huge incalculability of size and tallness in height.

Figures moved within.

"That's it, isn't it," Lord Althalos asked Elisia, not diverting his eyes from the horrific, terrible all-feared sight that was unravelling before them.

"Yes, yes, it is."

"Raise your weapons, men," Borgian called out towards the crowd who immediately obeyed.

Evening came quickly, and the Malice of Snow had reached them in no time, Borgian held the Ethril Blade in his right hand.

"Are you going to be ok with the one hand?" Elisia asked.

"Yes, I'll be fine, I still have my sword hand, that's all I need."

Borgian gave Elisia a quick smile just before a dread-inflicting roar echoed across the sky, enough to disturb the gods in their domain.

The roar came from a giant shadow within the snow, which blotched out what remained of the setting sun.

Borgian recognised the creature, it was what he had seen in the pit of the Pearl Palace: The Revenant of the Pit, the one that the book told, would rise on reckoning day.

The beast was formed of bones and ice, and was bigger than any building or any city, its skeletal head reached into the clouds.

"What is it?" Terrowin questioned.

"The Revenant."

The beast stepped out from the snow, as the Disavowed stampeded from within, in a flood.

Borgian couldn't fathom in words, the size of the beast, everyone had forgotten about it and it would be a great mistake.

"Kill them all," the hollow voice of Rolgirtis sounded.

The armies of men moved into position, merging and forming a shield wall, these shields not made from Tritanhium, like their weapons.

The Disavowed began to jump from out of the snow, spearing the soldiers they landed on.

The shields, as expected, did nothing against the creatures, and froze and corroded as the snowstorm encapsulated the battle, in the end, they were abandoned, and they began to fight with more success, equipping their weapons, limb splitting the creatures.

Borgian became too distracted by their sudden success, to notice the Revenant as it slowly edged towards him and raised its colossal foot above his head.

"Run! Borgian, run!" Mazdol shouted out a warning from across the battlefield.

Borgian quickly realised the shadow that loomed above and began to run, jumping before the foot smashed down, moving the earth beneath it and making the ground tremble.

Borgian speedily snatched up the Ethril Blade from the ground in just enough time to stab it through the hip of a Disavowed approaching him.

Borgian turned around to see a large puddle of red blood gather from under the Revenant's foot where the soldiers had been squashed flat and exploded.

Borgian turned back around to see Elisia struggling on the floor, he rushed to help her up.

"It seems what they say is true, the battlefield really isn't a place for women," she exclaimed before quickly equipping a Tritahnite dagger from the floor, and like a dart, aiming at a Disavowed behind Borgian, directly hitting its eye.

"I take back what I said, the battlefield is a place for women," she disappeared back into the battle and left Borgian to fend off two oncoming Disavowed.

They advanced on Borgian from either side, closing in on him, they both struck at once and Borgian ducked, his sword then lit up and blinded the creatures, allowing Borgian enough time to recover himself and slaughter one of the Disavowed.

When he turned around to dispatch of the other, he was caught off guard, the Disavowed pulled its arm back and then punched forward, its spear of flesh stabbing into Borgian's stomach.

Borgian fell to the floor, winded and in more pain than he'd ever felt before.

He felt himself bleeding out.

He saw himself bleeding out.

"Borgian!" Mazdol shouted out from nearby, stabbing many Disavowed as he progressed towards Borgian, "what in hell have you done!"

Mazdol drove his sword through the hip of one of the Disavowed, and its inners spewed out over the snow.

Mazdol looked upon Borgian's wound, it was a large gaping hole filled with blood and lost entrails that emptied onto the ground below.

"Testudo formation," Mazdol boomed as the Disavowed fell to the floor.

A group of soldiers, the only group left to have working shields, quickly sped towards Borgian and Mazdol, creating a structure of shield walls and roof over them.

Mazdol inspected Borgian further, now that he was protected from the battle, the spear really had gone straight through Borgian's body.

There was nothing Mazdol could do.

Borgian's eyes rolled back into his head, and the Ethril Blade began to glow once more, but brighter than before.

Mazdol, stricken with grief after losing his best friend, found the strength to inspect the blade.

When he touched it, he found it burnt his hand, and then the blade began to crack.

The source of the light within the blade escaped and fled from the Testudo formation.

Mazdol was left with the shards of the broken blade and the corpse of his friend.

Suddenly, the shield wall collapsed, a Disavowed had come knocking, and easily moved the soldiers aside.

Mazdol quickly collected the shards of the blade, just in case, and stashed them in his knapsack.

He readied his blade as the Disavowed loomed over him.

He boomed a cry of battle.

Borgian quickly got up, a layer of ice lay below him, he very nearly slipped as he mounted the ground and rebalanced himself.

He looked down abruptly, remembering the devastating wound the Disavowed had made in his stomach region.

There was no wound.

Borgian inspected what was around him and noticed how high up he was, he looked over the edge of the icy structure and saw clouds, and below that, the battle that raged on.

He recognised where he was, he was standing on the Revenant's frozen skull.

How he was alive was a mystery to him, as it would be to any other person seeing him.

How he had got up here, he was also unaware of an answer.

"Confused?" a voice suggested behind him.

Borgian quickly turned around to identify who had spoken.

It was no other than the Blue Knight, Rolgirtis.

"The Ethril Blade is gone, it lies in pieces, and so do you, Borgian," Rolgirtis edged slightly towards him, "what you are now is the product of two malformed pieces of souls trying to reattach, one from the blade, one from your body, all you are missing is the piece from my blade, it's why you're still on this earth, because your soul can't detach from this world, it's missing a part of itself that draws near."

Rolgirtis unsheathed the Sword of Fading, the blade holding the last part of Borgian's soul, keeping him away from ultimate death.

Rolgirtis moved towards Borgian faster, this time, "When I kill you, this time, you will die and the last of your soul will merge with my sword, I will be invincible, and the Malice of Snow will be unstoppable."

Borgian moved back across the length of the Revenant's skull.

Rolgirtis moved forward, drawing his sword back, readying his blade for it to be plunged into Borgian.

Borgian continued to move backwards, watching his step, but then a hand grasped his leg, it was a hand of ice protruding from the base of the Revenant's skull.

More followed, some more extensive than others, all held tight to Borgian, lifting him into the perfect position for Rolgirtis to strike him.

Borgian prepared himself but soon found the hilt of a cold blade in hand as Rolgirtis approached.

Borgian used the blade to smash the hands holding him back.

He managed to free himself and could sense Rolgirtis' fury.

This time he approached Rolgirtis.

"Borgian's dead, the blade's in pieces," Mazdol told Zensi hesitantly.

"Sorry, what?" Zensi exclaimed.

"He was caught off guard by a Disavowed and then after he died, the blade shattered."

"Then, we're doomed, truly," Zensi announced, "do you have the shards?"

"Yes," Mazdol replied.

"I hate to do this, but we may not have another choice," Elisia stated.

Elisia caught her general as he walked past her, "Tell them to fall back, the battle is lost."

"Are you sure?" The general asked.

"Yes, fall back," Zensi confirmed.

The general lost himself in the battle and began yelling the command.

Horns sounded, announcing the retreat.

Zensi was approached by several soldiers after the command was given.

"We can't fall back, my queen, the Disavowed have formed a wall around the battle."

"Then, break the wall," Zensi commanded.

"No, it can't be done, the Disavowed are frozen in place, the ice is unbreakable, if anything, it strengthens with every hit we try."

"Then, we fight till death, it is glorious to die in battle," Zensi stated before vanishing into the crowd.

The snow was no longer white, it was completely red from where it had absorbed and retained the colour of the blood that had flooded it in the past two hours.

Fear overwhelmed the minds of the soldiers, a stench of terror whirled around the area, sweat stung the eyes of warriors.

A miasma of putrid smells, flesh and bodies.

The only thing to cool the soldiers down was their own sticky blood, as it froze to their skin in the cold.

Men screamed in agony, obscuring the still deafening sound of weapons thundering against armour.

The fatigue of the armies sealed their fates, the armours began to over-encumber, and people began to asphyxiate, not being able to breathe due to their throats becoming clogged with mixtures of mucus and blood.

Death flowered and bloomed.

The field soon became full of the roses of demise.

Everything had led up to this, all the deaths, all the journeys that Borgian had travelled.

He would win, or he would die.

And he couldn't die or everything he, and everyone else had sacrificed, would be for nothing.

The fate of Askaria was in this final battle, the fate of Askaria was on Borgian's shoulders.

Borgian hoped the responsibility would not weigh him down.

He smelt the blood.

He felt the cold.

He saw Rolgirtis as he tried an attack...

Borgian dodged swiftly and lifted the Ethril Blade for further defence.

"Do you think that now that you have summoned a blade, you will be victorious, no such luck befalls mortal men," Rolgirtis announced, "especially, when they decide they are going to fight a god."

"You are no god, Rolgirtis, just a weak man who stole the powers of one."

Rolgirtis and Borgian then attacked at the same time.

Their blades clashed and lit up, a great light illuminated the struggle above and the battle below.

Borgian noticed that the longer the blades touched for, the less bright Rolgirtis' sword became and the brighter Borgian's did.

The Ethril Blade was re-consuming Borgian's soul from the Sword of Fading.

Rolgirtis also noticed this and quickly detached his sword from Borgian's.

Borgian knew what he had to do know and continued to touch his blade to Rolgirtis'.

Rolgirtis then raised his blade in his two hands and sent out a burst of light.

The battle had, all of a sudden, ceased, the wall of the Disavowed around the battle had broken and the Disavowed retreated to the Revenant.

Zensi decided she was going to take this chance, "Fall back! Fall back!" she shouted out.

They hadn't won, but they hadn't lost either.

What they had lost however were thousands and thousands of soldiers.

The ground was painted red, the blood, and patterned black, the soldiers.

The armies retreated.

Borgian had known what Rolgirtis had done, he had called for backup.

Many of the Disavowed were scaling the structure of the Revenant, they were coming for him.

Borgian had little time to prepare himself, he hit Rolgirtis' sword one more time and absorbed more power than he had before.

The Ethril Blade glowed amazingly bright, it lit up the sky like a huge, near star.

The Disavowed began to mount the Revenant and started to run at Borgian.

Rolgirtis allowed his mutated army to do the work for a moment, a mistake.

Borgian carved through the Disavowed with a sudden strength he had never known was within him.

He had a feeling the power of the sword was finally being unleashed.

And soon, the Ethril Blade began to set the enemy ablaze.

The blue fire spread amongst the Disavowed.

They no longer posed a challenge.

The Disavowed parted to reveal Rolgirtis speeding towards Borgian.

"You're learning how to use the blade, now, aren't you, Borgian?" Rolgirtis realised, "perhaps, this fight will be a little more interesting than I thought."

Rolgirtis raised his blade above his head and slammed it down.

The Ethril Blade created a shield of ice over Borgian and protected against the blow from Rolgirtis.

The battle had really begun.

Borgian, filled with a new confidence, fought furiously against Rolgirtis who still handled him with ease.

The snow began to pick up to the point where it began to blind Borgian.

Rolgirtis knocked Borgian down and when he got up, he could no longer see Rolgirtis as he crept behind him, in the snowstorm.

Borgian used his blade to light the area so that he could see his foe, and then from out of nowhere, Rolgirtis attacked.

Borgian dropped the Ethril Blade in surprise and quickly crawled to reclaim it as Rolgirtis proceeded to get rid of Borgian, once and for all.

Rolgirtis equipped his sword in two hands and raised it above Borgian and as he plunged it downwards, Borgian rolled onto his front to reveal the Ethril Blade in front of his chest.

The Sword of Fading hit the Ethril Blade and as it did, the last of its blue light faded out and it shattered into pieces.

A blue light escaped from the shards and was consumed by the Ethril Blade.

"What have you done?!" Rolgirtis shouted out in fury as his armour, his skin, his body began to disintegrate into the snow that swirled around the area.

He walked towards Borgian in anger, and with no weapon, just stood there in his last moments, "You've ruined everything, you will all burn when the fire rains."

A blue light emitted from Borgian's symbol on his hand again and collected a wisp from the remains of Rolgirtis: it was what remained of Borgian's soul apart from what of it that was contained in the shards of the Sword of Fading.

Borgian collected up the shards.

The Disavowed began to drop like flies, from the Revenant, and crumble, like Rolgirtis, and disappear into the snow.

The storm ceased, and the snow melted.

And the armies of men began to turn around towards the battlefield once more as the Revenant smashed into pieces.

The Ethril Blade cast a protective globe round Borgian as he fell slowly downwards.

The armies cheered and walked back towards the dying Revenant.

"Borgian?" Mazdol called out, confused.

Zensi also pulled a bewildered face and followed Mazdol, towards Borgian.

"You're alive?" Mazdol exclaimed.

"No," Borgian watched as the Ethril Blade in his hand evaporated into a blue light and relocated to a knapsack on Mazdol's hip just as it did from the symbol on his hand and the shards of the Sword of Fading.

His soul lay in the remains of the Ethril Blade now, his soul's vessel.

"No?" Zensi repeated, puzzled.

"I am a product of malformed parts of my soul, the last part resided in Rolgirtis' blade, and due to the fact, I died before it could reattach with the other parts of my soul, it can never reattach, it'll reside in the Ethril Blade now," Borgian explained.

Mazdol revealed the shards of the blade from his knapsack, "And here is the blade."

"So, you're invincible, you can't die," Zensi stated.

"Yes, in a way, unless the shards are rebuilt and given to another wielder, then Borgian's soul will be forced to leave, and Borgian will die," Elisia explained.

"So, we've won, Rolgirtis is dead, correct?" Mazdol wondered.

"Yes, he won't be coming back," Borgian announced.

Borgian looked around, he stood on bodies, they were piled high across the battlefield, as far as the eye could see.

The bloodied snow could be scarce seen, only through the small gaps between the bodies.

The armies returned to their cities to rest and drink, to eat, and spend money on taboo pleasures.

Borgian returned to Mezal with Mazdol, and Elisia and Zensi returned to their newly claimed city of Talgrin, but not before Mazdol stopped Zensi to whisper something in her ear, "Now, the real war begins, good luck."

"And good luck with your illness, Mazdol, everyone knows you're sick, everyone knows your vulnerable and people, powerful people, will join me, whilst you're vulnerable," Zensi whispered back, "I have your city and your children, your soldiers and your money, you're lost Mazdol."

Dear Borgian Steel,

As a matter of urgency, the Crowned Citadel requires yours, and all the lords of Askaria's attention, a great power has been defeated, and great powers, the Ethril Blade and the Sword of Fading, now need to be stored safely in our possession, this letter has been sent to all lords of Askaria, your attendance is absolutely necessary and to not attend is an illegal offence.

Two ships will be awaiting your arrival at the port of Hernight.

Yours faithfully,

Vergillius Penvale, Head of the Council Moot of Askaria, Parliament Leader of the Crowned Citadel

The letters were sent to every city in Askaria, spreading worry, the Council Moot were recognised as the most powerful people in Askaria, and whenever a meeting occurred, a big change was sure to occur afterwards, and little did the lords of Askaria know, but the Council Moot weren't just wanting the Ethril Blade but something more.

The people of Askaria would be right to fear, a big change *was* soon to occur.

CHAPTER 34
HERNIGHT

Hernight was a city near to where the battle had struck, it was the capital city of the borough that it resided in: The Cold.

The first thing that Borgian immediately saw when he looked at the city were the hundreds of tents established outside the of it—the Missionary camps.

Borgian met with the Lords of the city just outside the camps.

"Gods, it's like a siege," Mazdol exclaimed.

"That's pretty much what it is, an army blockading people in a city until they give into their terms," Borgian commented.

Aminucilie spoke, "I used to be friends with Lord Aramor until this whole fiasco escalated to this point, I told him to just give in, pretend, but still continue to worship his gods ... he didn't listen and now he's facing the consequences."

The lords advanced into the midst of the Missionaries' camp, they were surrounded by people dressed in grey robes and silver masks who stared at them as they passed.

The Missionaries were like an organised army, they were forging weapons and armour, practising battle and holding rallies and speeches about religion and war.

"Funny how those two things seemed to cross over so commonly," Borgian thought.

Borgian had heard of the Missionaries' island, or islands, they were known as The Eye and The Mouth and were connected by a bridge, they held a palace of worship, a town and boasted the largest navy in all of Askaria and the continent of Magnathoth.

They approached the gate to Hernight and it was opened by a group of soldiers dressed in light grey armour.

They surrounded a man with heavy bags under his eyes, a silver crown on his head and long jet-black hair beneath his crown: he was Lord Aramor Benortitien.

"Nice to have people knocking on my door who don't have the intention of harassing me or trying to force me to follow a religion that I don't believe in, let's get going," Aramor turned on heel towards the back of his city where another large gate was embedded in the wall.

Hernight was a dark and miserable place, it's walls were so high, they blocked out the scarce amount of sunlight that the citadel had been gifted, and the people; so dismal and tired, their skin seemed to have invited a tone of pastel grey to settle there.

A mist seeped in through the crevices in the walls and the clouds looming overhead were dull like stone.

The buildings were small and quaint, formed of a mixture of wood and grey concrete to go with the faces of the people and the overall gloom that surrounded the city.

"So, Aramor, have you managed to obscure or fend off the Missionaries in any way so far?" Mazdol asked dumbly.

"Does it look like I have, Mazdol, I wasn't aware your illness caused you to go blind of everything going on around you," Aramor retorted suddenly.

"You know about my illness too?" Mazdol questioned, uncertainly.

"Everyone knows Mazdol, half of the doctors you hire arrive through my port," Aramor told.

There was a smog hanging over Hernight from the fires of the Missionary camps, and a silence over the lords.

It was an uncomfortable one that was eventually broken by Elisia, "How long is it to the Crowned Citadel?"

"You don't know?" Aramor said, surprised.

"No, I've never been before, my husband attended the meetings, I was never invited," Elisia spoke sadly, remembering her husband.

"Oh my, Elisia Clairn, please excuse me, I didn't recognise you at first," Aramor apologised before turning to shake hands with Elisia.

She took it, she needed as many friends in this war, now everyone knew of her allegiance to Zensi in the War of the Crown.

Eventually, they arrived at the port, the two ships awaited them along with a group of soldiers in heavy bronze armours and masked, gladiator-like helmets.

"If all lords could proceed to the ship on the right, and Borgian Steel, to the ship on the left," one of the soldiers gave demands.

"Why am I going on this ship, have we got a problem?" Borgian inquired.

"We found a letter within the city that, when decoded, entailed that a plot to capture you is soon to take place, this is for your safety."

CHAPTER 35
ENDING A WAR

In total, they ended up waiting about half an hour in front of the walls of crowned turrets and beyond that, towers, for Borgian and the second ship to arrive.

Hope was lost in the end and a patrol of guards was posted to stay vigilant of Borgian.

The lords couldn't waste any more time, they were escorted through the heavily guarded Crowned Citadel, to the tallest tower where the First Crown was guarded and the most powerful man in Askaria: Vergillius Penvale, head of the Council Moot of Askaria and protector of the First Crown, resided.

He was a man that Mazdol knew much about, his father and Vergillius were friends a long time ago mainly due to the fact that they were both well-off.

Vergillius came from the wealthiest family in the eastern land of the Blacklands, who had become rich from their many businesses in writing, warfare and global trade.

The Crowned Citadel, where they currently resided, was located on a small island north of Askaria and directly above Hagmars Wall.

It was a city with no people, forbidden to all except those in the Council Moot or the lords when a meeting was due.

The gate opened by two levers that required keys to be able to be used.

The citadel was formed entirely of towers made from a dull yet beautiful orange sandstone.

It was a safe haven and with no one around, was the most peaceful place imaginable.

The sea could be heard from outside the walls, waves lapping against the jagged cliffs of the island that the city was mounted upon.

The sound of the sea set all the lords wondering where exactly on the sea, Borgian was.

Was he lost? Had his ship been taken over by pirates or had he been captured by the threat Elisia had heard one of the soldiers talking about, as they boarded their ship?

The soldiers that the group followed, took them to the tallest tower of all before disappearing off into the city.

The tower was guarded by a circle of soldiers with their shields facing outwards, and then another circle behind that.

The soldiers removed themselves out of the way so that the lords could pass through into the door-less tower.

A couple of guards resumed the job of escorting the lords, from within, to their next destination.

The inside of the tower was odd-looking in the way that it looked very narrow from the outside and was extremely spacious on the inside, with a grand staircase centring everything.

On the walls were portraits of previous heads of the Council Moot on one side, and previous Arch Kings on the other side.

The staircase in the middle, they ascended, and were led to another spacious room with a huge table, with two men and one woman sat on it, just off centre.

"Borgian?" Was the first word Vergillius spoke upon everyone taking their seats.

"We don't know," Zensi replied.

"Does he have the Ethril Blade?" Vergillius asked with worry on his face despite the coolness in his voice.

Mazdol tossed the knapsack, containing the Ethril Blade shards, onto the table, "No."

"As resourceful as your father," Vergillius remarked, picking up the knapsack and handing it to the man sitting next to him who proceeded up the stairs with it.

"I'm supposing that wasn't all you wanted to see us for," Althalos assumed.

"Correct," Vergillius confirmed, "if any of you remember, a long time ago, a deal was made between me, Zensi and Mazdol."

"Shit," Mazdol suddenly exclaimed, knowing what was coming.

"In 3A 286, the year that Zensi declared war on Mazdol, the year that we found a suitable heir who, however, was not Askarian—the deal was struck because the people wanted an Askarian leader, and so Zensi was chosen, however the crown was torn between her and Mazdol and could not choose, so eleven years were given for one to kill the other, so the crown could choose," Vergillius explained, "the deal was if one wasn't dead before the deadline, then the heir we had chosen before, would be elected."

"And who is this heir?" Elisia enquired.

"King Valenmir Ravenscar, son of the ruler of the Blacklands, Baron of Raven's Breach," Vergillius announced proudly, "he has been considered for years, and now his time has come."

"Couldn't you extend the deadline?" Mazdol suggested.

"Eleven years, I gave you Mazdol, and you and Zensi did nothing with them and you will continue to do nothing, the Council Moot's elite assassins will be targeted towards you if you dare proclaim war against each other again."

"What if the First Crown doesn't lend itself to Valenmir? What then? What if the crown has become accustomed to Zensi and

225

Mazdol? I've read about similar things happening before in the past, it's not uncommon," Aramor wondered aloud.

"Then we cover up, forge a fake crown, the First Crown never accepted Corpulus, he wore a fake crown all his life and it changed nothing."

"What?" Mazdol exclaimed.

"And there's the truth of it, the First Crown is beyond men and mer, it isn't just a piece of metal, it is a being of choice and knowledge, created by the first lords, Ask and Embla, and the races of Dvergr and the Haltija," Vergillius held, "Valenmir will arrive on the first day of the following year."

Elisia walked from the Citadel, accompanied by Zensi, they re-boarded the boat they had arrived on and Elisia took her place by the side of the ship.

She stared off the edge, into the sea.

She looked at her reflection and saw something in the distance behind her, a bird, a magpie on the crow's nest.

Elisia looked behind herself as the bird flew down to meet her gaze, it opened its beak to reveal its many rows of teeth.

Elisia jumped back in terror.

It was the magpie she had seen before Bolgron and disaster struck there, was disaster going to strike again?

Soon enough, Askaria re-appeared on the horizon.

Elisia wondered where Borgian was, where Askaria would take her next and what terror awaited her past the borders she was about to enter.

A new king was to rise.

A new danger to take hold.

Tears of Fire to rain.

EPILOGUE
TEARS OF FIRE

Borgian awakened.

He had been blinded by a black piece of material over his eyes.

He could smell the metallic miasma of blood and the smoke of fires.

He could hear footsteps, and metal being sharpened—a grindstone whirring as it spun and emitting a grating sound as weaponry touched it.

Fire crackling...

He could feel the presence of dismay lingering.

"What do you want? Who are you?" Borgian asked, trying desperately to imbue confidence into his voice whilst he asked his questions.

Trying not to show the dread he felt.

"What I want to do relies on you being who you are, and that is the question you should be asking, 'Who am I for you to want to kidnap me?' And who you are, Borgian 'Steel' Veles, is the sacrifice, for the dragon."

Born 2004 in Gloucester, Callum Paul Higgins is the Stroud-based #1 Amazon bestselling author of the First Crown series who released his debut novel, First Crown: Malice of Snow, in March and April last year, and marshaled into the epic fantasy writing industry to much success, carried by his hard work and commitment, his global fandom and unique story.

At present, he is the youngest published author in Gloucestershire, with a keen interest in furthering the trend of young people fulfilling their dreams and defying stereotypes.

He has been, locally, on BBC Radio Gloucestershire and has been featured in Gloucester and Stroud Citizen, the Gloucester Review, Stroud News and Journal, Gloucestershire Live, the Local Answer, as well as being supported by large entities; supermarket chain, Tesco, and cafe chain, Coffee #1.

Outside of this, he has been interviewed for Teenage Cancer Trust, as well as CALI magazine and Armada Reviews, in the US, and Das Gespräch, in Germany, as well as many writing blogs and press where he has been critically awarded for his unique style of writing, and entrance into a competitive industry, at only 14.

He has met with Stroud's MP, David Drew, and has dipped his toes into business and politics, activism and the empowering of youth on many occasions.

Callum's political alignment is central-left and believes in people power above everything.

He also strongly believes in and supports equal rights for the LGBTQ+ community and stresses that the views of many faiths and peoples, against them, are utterly outdated, irrelevant and lacking in real understanding and compassion.

He also believes in activism for our environment, being crippled by not only us, the people, but by pure idiocy and laziness from those above.

In the past, he has also worked alongside the Teenage Cancer Trust, donating 20% of his book profits to their cause, and is an ambassador for OCD-UK.

He is also the founder of a unique publishing company, Askaria Publishing, and the Talgrin Project which is a heavily backed fund of Callum's creation, which supports young people against the many issues they may be faced with, including discrimination.

Callum currently lives in Stroud, Gloucestershire, near the village of Lypiatt.

callumhiggins.site123.me

askariapublishing.site123.me

Printed in Poland
by Amazon Fulfillment
Poland Sp. z o.o., Wrocław